The Compound

Ann R. Halstead

PublishAmerica
Baltimore

First printing

ISBN: 1-60836-598-0
PUBLISHED BY PUBLISHAMERICA, LLLP
www.publishamerica.com
Baltimore

Printed in the United States of America

This book is dedicated to my husband Bill. Thank you for encouraging me to follow my dreams and write my first book.

1

Joe finished painting the last of the latches and hooking up the electrical for the new camera. 'Now I have another angle to watch those critters,' he thought.

Coming through the woods, Sophie saw something out of the corner of her eye.

"Jack, look over there! It's a family of rabbits."

Joe looked in the direction Sophie was pointing. "Walk lightly you'll scare them off."

"I know." Sophie gave Jack a look.

As they walked up to the rabbits, not a one stirred. It was like they were all trained to sit, until commanded to move. Sophie saw what she thought was a larger rabbit and some babies, they were huddled together near a large boulder. She walked over and knelt down. The female rabbit was large, very large. It had deep amber eyes shaped like a cats eyes not a rabbits. It was laying there hunched up like a ball. The babies were surrounding the older animal; they looked like full grown hamsters.

Sophie knelt down to get a closer look. "Oh my, look at this." She reached out to touch one of the babies. As she touched it, it moaned, like it was in pain. Sophie jerked her hand back and stood up.

"That was weird. I wonder what's wrong with them." Sophie said.

"Come on, let's go. We might catch Joe before he leaves. Besides, something's not right with those little critters."

Jack took Sophie's hand and they started towards the house. It was out in the middle of nowhere, from where they parked the car, to the house it was about 1/4 mile. There were no stairs or walkway, so they just had to walk through the woods up to the house.

"What I wonder is why the driveway stops here at the car and doesn't go up to the house?" Jack said.

"Yea, that is a good question, I would hate to carry the groceries up to the house."

"Think about this, what if it was raining or snowing, that would be a bitch." Jack grabbed Sophie's hand and they walked up the hill.

"How did Joe find this place? It's so serine and beautiful. The air is so fresh."

About the time Sophie commented on the surroundings, they heard a noise. Jack turned around to find two cats, or were they cats, following them. They looked odd, like a tall black domestic cat with long ears. The shape of it body was like an hour glass. The face was small and elongated. And the fur was like that of a rabbit. They followed with a hop and a run, like a mix of the rabbit and wild cat, and they were following Jack and Sophie.

"I wonder what they are." Jack said. "They don't seem to be unfriendly. Just following us at a distance, being cautious I guess."

"Aren't those the little rabbits we saw back there?" Sophie asked.

"I don't know, the ones back there were all huddled together."

"They are kind of neat looking, maybe even a little scary." Sophie added.

Walking through the woods was very relaxing, but very mysterious. Sophie kept looking around feeling something was watching her, and those cats, or what ever they were, following behind was becoming annoying.

"I wonder why they're following us?" Sophie asked.

"I don't know, what I do know is I am hungry and want to get up to the house."

"You're always hungry."

They heard scuttling and something moving in the woods, but that was normal wasn't it? Birds, squirrels and other animals lived in the woods and this was their home, they had a right to be here.

"Let's pick up the pace," Jack said, "It is getting dark out fast, and I'm kind of creeped out a bit.

Everything got very quiet all of the sudden. They stopped walking and just listened. They looked around and the strange animals were gone.

"Lets go." Sophie sounded nervous.

As they approached the compound, as Joe called it, they noticed something strange. There was a mote of sorts dug around the house, not deep, but deep enough. Coming up from the ravine were metal spikes, as sharp as swords. They were placed about a foot apart in all directions. If the sun was not going down so fast and it was a little lighter out they would have seen the dark red stains on some of the spikes.

"What the hell..."

"This is weird," Sophie said, "and the day gets even stranger"

"Well let's go find out what the mystery is all about. Joe has some explaining to do. I wonder what he has gotten us into this time."

Joe was always the one in their group of friends that always stumbled on some really strange stuff. Last summer at the beach there was this strange fog and mean as crap snapping turtles. The three of them had to run for their lives. The winter before that they were skiing in Aspen. A snow hermit was trying to hunt them down and kill them because they were skiing on his mountain. They never figured out why he didn't go after all the other people that were skiing on "his" mountain. There was always an adventure when Joe was around.

No matter what was going on at the time, Joe was always coming up with a plan, and surprisingly, with some effort and most of the time a trip to the hospital, Joe got the job done.

Sophie and Jack followed the mote around to the front of the house. The surroundings were all natural. No pretty flowers or ornamental trees or bushes. The porch was a plain decked porch but there were wires around all the window and door casings. The stairs going up to the porch were metal, almost like an escalator, but not moving. Above the windows were rolled up sheets of metal.

The front door opened abruptly as Jack and Sophie climbed the hollow sounding staircase.

"Well it's about time you two got here; did you find the compound o-k?" Joe looked excited to see his friends. He seemed to age since last summer at the beach. Through his big smile Sophie noticed the creases in his forehead. 'He sure looks like he has been under a lot of stress,' she thought.

Sophie took a few steps in to the house and gave Joe a big hug. "It is so beautiful out here, how did you ever find this place?" Jack stepped in behind her and dropped their duffle bag and slammed the door.

"So, what's the mystery this time?"

"Jack, don't be so mean. We just got here. Joe has invited us out to this beautiful place in the woods to relax. Now, relax."

Joe acted surprised at the question, almost hurt. With a sly smile he said, "I have a little animal problem here at the compound. I tell you about it a little later."

2

The compound. Joe bought the property and the house on it from old man Sloan. It set in the Smokey Mountains of Tennessee. It is said that Sloan owned the property, about 500 acres of land. Little by little the county bought a parcel of the land from Sloan as he needed the money. They then added it to the national forest so that no one else could live on the land. Sloan raised hell every time he had to sell a chunk. He believed the government was after him and the rest of the nation, buying up land, taking control.

He never had a job, just one lucky mountain man that inherited the land a long time ago. In 2005 he found out he had cancer; he didn't want the county to get the land so he sold it to the highest bidder and moved onto a nursing home until he died a year later. What he didn't disclose at the closing was, the woods had some very strange animals and some very strange things happened when there was a full moon. No one knew that he had been doing artificial insemination on those strange animals. If he ever told anyone that, he would have been committed.

Sloan was somewhat of a scientist. He liked to compound chemicals, and use the animals in the woods in the experiments. He was a little crazy. Sloan wanted to make his mark on the world. He figured if he cross bred two animals and give them some of his formula he could breed miniature unique animals that people would enjoy having. He would make a fortune. Well the formula went bad, bad things happened. Then the cancer came. The old man developed a form of cancer that quickly robbed him of his memory and his life.

After he sold the property to Joe, he had no where to go. Sloan checked himself in to a nursing home. His mind and body deteriorated fast. By then it was too late to tell anyone about the experiments he had performed on the animals. He had forgotten.

All of Sloan's furniture and equipment was left behind. The man left with the clothes on his back.

When Joe started the cleanup of the house and property, just about everything in the lab was trashed, even the journals. At the time it was thought to be all trash.

After a year of cleanup and refurbishing the house, Joe moved in. For about a year there were no problems. An occasional bear or raccoon would get into the trash; Joe learned the ways of the wildlife and made a few adjustments to keep the critters out. What he didn't expect were the strange cats.

People say strange things happen on the night of a full moon, Joe knows first hand about those things.

3

Joe gave Jack a guy hug and a welcoming slap on the back. "Its great to see you guys. After last Summer I thought you guys would never talk to me again."

"We thought about it" Jack said kidding around.

"Oh stop it Jack, you know we love you Joe, it's always great to see you." Sophie said.

"I'm glad you two decided to come up and stay at the compound while I am away. I am going to leave in a couple of days, so we will have time to visit, catch up on old times and I will even show you around. There is more that meets the eye up here." 'Such an understatement,' Joe thought.

"So how long are you going to be on this little Boy Scout adventure?" asked Jack.

"Just a week and it's not the Boy Scouts," Joes face turned a little red, "just me and a couple of guys heading up the mountain to get back to nature, you know camp, hunt and live off the land."

"You're such a man!" Sophie teased. "So Joe, I'm curious, what's up with the mote, the spikes...and all the other strange stuff around here? Now I know why you call this a compound."

"It's for protection, I have been having a little problem certain times of the month with the local fare around here."

Jack rolled his eyes, "Oh no! Here we go again. Joe why did you really invite us up here in the middle of no where? What are you up to now?"

Sophie, feeling a little nervous again said, "What do you mean the "local fare"?"

"Well I figure I have to eat them before they eat me." Joe started laughing. "Just kidding it's not that bad. It just gets a little crazy around here on a full moon. And so I needed someone to watch the place while I am gone."

Jack was not impressed, he knew Joe, they grew up together, friends since childhood. To Joe nothing was that serious, and then it got worse. He seemed to attract trouble. Sometimes damn right strange trouble. If Jack wasn't involved in half the shit Joe got himself into, he wouldn't believe it ever happened.

Now Joe was loosing patience. "What do you mean a full moon and craziness? What is going on here? Are we in danger? And about that mote and spikes, wired up windows and the stairs? What else are you going to come up with?"

"Don't worry so much, it's all under control, trust me!"

Jack mumbled under his breath..."'Trust me,' he says. The last time I trusted you I almost got myself killed by sick sea turtles, I still don't believe they were turtles. Heck! I still don't believe...well never mind. Tell me what the story is this time."

Sophie piped up and asked, "When is the next full moon?"

"You believe this shit, it's not Halloween, and Joe is just trying to be funny."

Sophie got up," I can't take this right now, I am starving, where is the kitchen?" Joe pointed down the hall.

"Hey Soph... I went to town yesterday; there is plenty of food in the pantry and in the fridge. Make your self at home"

"I always do," And Sophie took off down the hall.

4

"I'm curious Joe, What made you decide to move out to the middle of nowhere?"

"Well, I didn't really plan to live here. I just wanted a little place in the mountains, you know a get away. After mom and dad died and left me all that money, it seemed like a good deal. I got a great price on the land and the house, so I bought it. I didn't feel up to working, I needed a break. So I decided to take the time, fix up the place and stay a while. My boss at the dealership said I was welcome back any time. So when I'm ready I can go back. So here I am. After a while weird stuff started happening, and I had to keep adding to the compound to keep out the critters. Needless to say I'm still here."

Jack looked at Joe, "So what is going on?"

"I know this is going to sound crazy, and it is, but about six months ago, I finally got this place cleaned up on the inside. I went outside to clear the area around the house. I kept hearing strange noises. It was like an animal was hurt and moaning. Then there were the movements behind me, and when I turned around to look I didn't see anything. I thought it was my imagination. I felt like I was being watched. Then one day I was out chopping wood from an old tree that fell and I saw them. These cat like things were sitting just beyond the tree line watching me. I was watching them too, I didn't know what they were, I blinked and they were gone. Then I heard the sound again, that moaning, like someone or something was hurt. I have to admit it kind of freaked me out a bit."

"I think we may have seen a family of them in the woods on the hike up here. They looked like a cross between a rabbit and a funny shaped cat. The body was strange, shaped like an hourglass. Sophie thought they were rabbits. I thought they were cats. There were several of then huddled up near a large boulder. She went over to see them, they just lay there, and when she touched one it made that same noise."

"She did what? She touched one? Man, that's not good, she has the scent on her now. Let's talk outside. I guess I will have to come clean a little earlier than I wanted to. I just hope we don't have problems tonight."

"I knew there was going to be some reason you wanted us here."

"Jack, let me explain."

Jack followed Joe outside, "What do you mean? What's going on?"

"When I first saw the creatures I thought they were feral cats, maybe crossbred to take on there strange shape. Then one day I found one of their kittens, for lack of a better term, in the woods. It seemed to be lost or abandoned and hungry. I felt sorry for it and picked it up. I was just going to feed it and let it roam around the compound; you know kill mice and such. Big mistake." Joe took a deep breath. "No sooner than I picked it up I was almost surrounded by ten or twelve of these things, they all started moaning and crying, I put the kitten down. I slowly backed away from the pack. One of them started toward the kitten, picked it up and joined the pack. Then there was the most God awful noise I ever heard, they all started screaming at once, then they ran off in the woods. I think I stayed in the house for a week trying to figure out what to do."

Jack looked at Joe as if he were going nuts.

"What, you don't believe me?" Joe asked

Jack looked at Joe again, but it was getting dark and he couldn't see out into the woods any longer. He could feel eyes on him. 'No way, this is crazy. Joe is just freaking me out,' he thought. Jack was trying to hide it but he was getting very nervous.

"I'm afraid to ask, is that what all this protection is about?"

"You haven't seen anything yet." Joe said with a little excitement in his voice. "I'm debating, do I show this to you now or do we eat first and do this all together?"

"Let's go eat first; I may not have an appetite later. Joe, if Sophie or I get hurt because of one of your little schemes I'm going to be pissed."

"Don't worry, everything is under control. As long as you know what to do when I am gone everything will be fine. Besides I will be here through the full moon. The only thing I worry about is that Sophie touched one of them, and now the scent is in the house again."

"Is that bad? Can't she just go wash her hands or something?" Jack asked.

"It's too late for that, I just hope they don't think one

of there young is in the compound again, or we are going to have problems. Just in case we will lock up tonight, just to be safe."

Jack just looked at him and said, "Shit, here we go again."

5

Sophie whipped up a quick dinner of soup and sandwiches. They all sat down at the table to eat a bite.

"What were you two talking about outside? You know I can't be left out. I hope I didn't miss anything." Taking a bite of the sandwich Sophie looked at the two guys with interest.

"You didn't miss a thing," Joe said, "I was telling Jack about a little about what was going on here. After dinner I will tell you both about the weird problems and my security measures around here. Then I will take you on the ten cent tour."

"It looks like more than ten cents has been spent around here."

"Your right, more like ten thousand."

During dinner they talked about last summer at the beach.

Joe looked at Jack, "So how is the knee?"

"It's getting better, the doc says I need to exercise it more, just a bad muscle strain, but it seems like it is taking forever to heal."

Sophie looked annoyed, "No the Doc said you might need surgery, but men are such babies. Jack thinks he is a doctor and he knows best. So he is taking vitamins and glucosamine to fix the problem. Tell him Jack, is it working?"

"Sure it is, as long as I don't do too much."

"Such a baby."

"Alright you two, be nice." Joe felt a little guilty about the accident.

6

Last summer the three of them went to Hilton Head for a week vacation, Joe was supposed to meet an old flame, but that never happened. Well it would have if they didn't get caught up in the fog and confusion.

The three of them met at the condo at five in the afternoon. They unloaded their suitcases in their rooms and met up in the living room. Sophie fixed herself a drink and the guys popped a beer. They only saw each other twice a year, so they sat down and talked about all the things they were doing at home and at work. After another drink, they decided to take a walk on the beach.

The sun was starting to set and it was a beautiful site. The water was unusually still. They planned to walk for about an hour and then walk over to the Salty Dog and grab a drink before dinner. As they were walking back to the condo, the wind picked up a bit and waves starting rolling in. Looking out over the ocean a fog was rapidly coming towards the shore line. It looked ominous. They turned around to head back towards the condo. By the time they reached the property the fog had caught up with them, they could barely see ten feet in front of themselves.

As the story goes or the authorities wanted everyone to believe a pack of wild dogs was loose on the island. When the dense fog came in they came out to hunt for food. People could not see them because of the fog. They were going up to the vacationers and their pets and attacking them.

Jack and Joe did not see dogs, they didn't know what they saw, but it wasn't dogs.

Sophie didn't see anything at first; she just felt a nip on the back of her thigh. When she yelped from the pain, Jack turned around to see what was wrong. Sophie was kneeling down on the ground; tears started streaming down her face. Jack yelled to Joe for help, Joe didn't hear him at first because he had walked up ahead of them to give them a little privacy. Jack called to Joe a second time.

Jack saw something coming towards him, but he didn't quite know what it was, it wasn't a dog. It was larger than a dog but smaller than a deer. In the fog it looked like a giant sea turtle, but that was impossible, it was too big.

Joe finally heard Jack calling and started running back towards the beach. He couldn't see because of the fog. He ran off the path and lost his balance on the sand and sea oats. He went down. Joe screamed in pain, He felt something sting him or bite him, he wasn't sure which.

Jack and Sophie got up went running towards Joe, Jack tripped over him, falling and bashing his knee of a large piece of driftwood. He screamed out in pain and rolled onto the ground. That's how Jack hurt himself this time.

Finally, they made it back to the condo. Joe and

Jack were bleeding; Sophie had a nice bite on her thigh. Looking at it, the bite probably needed stitches. Joe checked out his wounds, he found strange bite marks and a few thorns. Jacks knee on the other hand, was swelling up like a watermelon.

On the way out the door to go to the emergency room, they grabbed some flashlights it was very dark and the fog was still thick. The scariest thing was the screaming. People were screaming everywhere. They rushed to the car and drove to the hospital. Traffic to get off the island was jammed. People were running scarred in the streets. Some were hurt but most were just frightened. A couple of times Joe had to slam on the breaks, people were running in front of the slow moving cars to get away from what ever was trying to get them.

As they drove up to the emergency room entrance there was a line of people a mile long. Jack got out at the entrance, because he couldn't walk well. Sophie helped him in the hospital. Joe parked the car and walked. People were moaning and crying in pain. The hospital was full to capacity.

The staff were doing the best they could with the hysterical people first, and the others would just have to wait their turn.

Everyone was speculating about what was going on. Some saw dogs, some saw giant turtles, somc saw big wild cats. It was all so surreal. Next thing you know the police were called in to call order to all the hurt people, it was a mad house.

Joe, Jack and Sophie finally left the hospital around nine am the next morning, stitched up, given shots and pain killers. They had to fill out massive amounts of paper work just in case the police or hospital needed to get in touch with them. Maybe the dogs were rabid. If that were the case they would need more medical attention.

As they left the hospital, the fog was gone and it was a beautiful day. That was the end of that vacation. They decided to head home the next day. They were in to much pain to enjoy themselves.

7

Joe wiped his mouth, "Great dinner Sophie, where did you learn to cook like that?"

"Ha ha, what you can't make soup and sandwiches? Sophie rolled her eyes, a bad habit she picked up from Joe.

"Well I guess it's about time I showed you two around. But before I do I have to tell you something important. This little trip I am going on...I am not really going away, I'm going on a little mission."

Jack looked at Sophie. "I told you, he is up to something."

"I'll be close to the compound; actually I'll be under the compound, for a little while anyway." Joe got up and motioned for Jack and Sophie to follow him. "We will start outside." Joe handed them flashlights, and walked towards the door.

"Is it safe to go out at dark?" Sophie asked

"Tonight it is. The critters, the bad critters, only come out to harm anyone and anything on a full moon and a new moon. That is why I have to trap and kill them."

Jack looked at Sophie with worried eyes. "So I guess we are here to help you?"

"In a way, yes. The critters try to get into the

compound when someone is here; it's like they know there is someone here and want to get in. From what I can tell they don't try to get in when I am not here. There is never any damage to the property when I am gone. The cats are mean and dangerous"

"Why are you getting us into another round of "Joe goes crazy"? Jack asked. "Every time the three of us get together, I get hurt.

"If I asked for help, would you really say no?"

Jack rolled his eye again, "No, I guess not. Well let's see what you got here."

"First I think I will show you the stairs, right inside the door is a switch, I painted it red, and it glows in the dark just in case. When you flip the switch, the stairs fold up into the casing under the porch."

"And why do you have disappearing stairs?" Sophie asked.

"Well these critters as I call them are very smart. Alright, let me come clean. These cat like animals are mutations. From what I understand, Sloan, the old man that lived here, was somewhat of a scientist. He did experiments on animals. He developed a plan to cross breed animals that shouldn't have been cross bred. The ones we are trying to get rid of are strange. I think it is part cougar, rabbit and who knows what else. I think it was a hobby of his. A strange hobby, but a hobby."

Jack looked puzzled, "Why would anyone want to do that, and why do they need to be 'gotten rid of'?"

"Well, I know this is going to sound a bit crazy, but, when there is a full moon and then the new moon, they feed. They want flesh, blood, and anything else they can eat. I think they smell humans as a food source. Soon after I moved in they have come straight here, the place where they were created. I don't know why they come here, but they do."

"Yes, that is crazy. Are you trying to scare us or what? Jack I think it is time for us to leave. I don't like this a bit." Sophie said.

Joe stopped Sophie, "Wait, let me finish. As far as we know, there are not too many left. But I still have to take precautions."

"O-k, now, who is we? Jack asked.

"There are a couple of houses up here spread apart, everyone has been having problems, and we have had some pretty close calls. So we have gotten together to exterminate the creatures."

Sophie, looking frightened, "Now they're creatures?"

"Look, I need some help, if you don't think you can help after I show you the rest, you can leave tomorrow. The full moon isn't till Friday." Joe started down the stairs.

The hollow sound of the stairs grated on Jacks nerves. They followed Joe into the yard.

Joe pointed the high beam flash light towards the mote and the spikes. "If you flip the blue switch, the mote fill up with water. The cats don't like water. When they try to jump over the mote, they can't get all the way across. Needless to say they fall on the spikes and die, hopefully."

"O-k, what happens if they make it across?" Jack asked.

"Well they can't get into the front door, because the stairs have been activated."

"I don't like this; it scares the crap out of me." Sophie looked back at the house, "What about the windows, and the porch, and the back door?"

"Come back in and I'll show you the rest" Jack and Sophie followed Joe back into the house.

"Some of the people who live up here are going to help me this weekend. We are going on a mission. It should be completed in three days. Then we can spend the rest of the week relaxing in the solitude of these beautiful mountains."

"So we have to work for our vacation again?" Jack said sarcastically.

"No like I said you can leave at day break if you don't like the plan. Come on; let me show you the rest."

Joe led Jack and Sophie thought the house to the kitchen. "See this black switch by the back door? Watch..." Joe flipped that switch and metal shutters came sliding out of the ceiling and covered the doors and windows in the whole house.

"WOW!" Jack and Sophie said at the same time. Jack asked, "How did you come up with that?"

"I watch a lot of the sci-fi channel. This is what keeps them out of the house, if they get across the mote. Now, follow me to see the best part."

Joe opened a door in the kitchen; it looked like any old pantry door. There were stairs going down, underneath the house, like a cellar. As they descended down, Joe was turning on the lights. It was dark and damp. The smell was overwhelming at first. The smell was of fresh turned dirt and something else Jack couldn't figure out. It was just a cellar; there was nothing down here but dirt, lights and wooden boxes.

"Joe what the hell, you have a couple of dozen boxes down here that look to me like gun boxes."

"They are, and with them we are going to get rid of

those cats once and for all. Come on." Joe started toward the front of the cellar.

As they looked ahead there was a tunnel carved into the wall of the cellar. Every couple hundred feet or so there was a gun box. Joe opened them; they were full of ammo and a few riffles. Some assault weapons and even grenades. Jack knelt down to check them out.

"This tunnel goes out to the end of the property, where you guys parked. Two nights from now me and a couple of my neighbors are going to go underground. The plan is when the cats come up to the house we are going to be in there rears, and blast them. You two are going to be at the house. At sundown Friday, the mission starts."

"Joe, what are we, the bait? You have got to be kidding. I am assuming you want us to be in the house to set the traps. Then you guys are going to trap them between yourselves and the house."

"Well you have part of it right. We aren't going to trap them. We are going to kill them." 'I just pray they don't get us first,' Joe thought.

Jack stopped walking, "Why don't the authorities get involved in this? Why are the good citizens of this mountain having to take matters into there own hands? This seems like a crazy plan to kill a couple of feral mutated cats."

"It's not a couple; we think there are about fifty or sixty, there were a lot more. We don't know how fast they breed." Joe admitted. "We go out every month and kill as many of them as we can. Last month we got about thirty."

"So what you are saying is they have reproduced,

hidden in the woods and no one sees them but two nights a month?" Sophie asked.

"No, you saw them. When you came up here, you saw them the way they are 29 days a month. Little cute rabbit like cat things, very docile. But when the moon is full they grow. Think of it his way. Remember the old tail of the werewolves. They are just mean dogs most of the time, then when the moon is full...need I say more?"

"You have lost your mind! You expect us to believe this crap. I think you have been alone in the woods for to long, you need a shrink, medication, or a padded cell." Jack lost his temper. "Prove it!"

8

"I have video. Is that proof enough?"

"Really?" Jack said.

"Two months ago Billy and Josh installed cameras for me. There are five of us involved in this mission. We all have our talents, and it works. I do most of the construction; you know the traps and planning how it all works. Billy and Josh are my brains, they do wiring, cable, computer monitoring, and trouble shooting. My closest neighbor is Gavin, he is a no fear kind of guy, He gets us the help we need doing the things we really can't or don't really want to do, like digging tunnels, or motes. He also is good at moral, a born leader as they say. Then there is Gage, He is young but strong. He also gets us the items we need to pull this off. He was Special Forces before he retired, then he won the lottery. So he not only has contacts, he has money. Gage wants our mountain back as much as we do.

Jack still didn't believe what was going on, "So those are your Boy Scouts, the ones who are going to risk there life to get rid of a few cats?"

After a long silence, Sophie popped up, "Jack, please calm down and let's go see this video. Joe is our friend and I think it is time to support him, besides;

we are going to be in the house and not out there with them. The least we can do is help pull a few switches and keep the door locked. Come on Joe let's get on with this, its getting late and I'm tired."

Jack on the brink of loosing it again said, "You have got to be kidding, how did you get so brave all of the sudden, I just can't..."

"Jack, Stop it!"

The three of them went upstairs to see the video. Joe led them into a downstairs den area. The place looked like command central. There were twelve monitors in a row, and keyboards for each monitor. On the wall by the door was a bank of switches, each color coded with labels. Joe fired up one of the computers and put a DVD into the computer. When it all started, there was a silence in the room.

What they saw was unbelievable. The tape kept switching from one part of the property to another. It showed small funny shaped cats walking up towards the house, as they came closer they were getting larger. They moved very slowly at first, almost like they were in pain, as they grew they became more agile and started running and pouncing.

These critters, as Joe called them started moaning and then howling. They were snapping at each other. Then they stopped, they heard something. On the video, Jack and Sophie heard a noise coming from a wooded area. The cats went looking for the noise. The camera panned over to the section of the property where the noise was coming from. All the cats, about twenty of them were breathing in the air; they smelled the deer that was hiding beyond the trees. The huge buck was grazing, he was a beautiful site.

His back to the house, he didn't see or here the cats creeping towards him. At the last possible moment they leaped and took down the buck.

Sophie jumped back and covered her mouth. She could not believe how fast it all happened.

Jack and Sophie watched as the cats feed on the buck, it was a gruesome site. They ripped it from limb to limb, there was blood everywhere. Everything happened in a matter of minutes.

"Well, have you seen enough?" Joe asked.

"My God, you weren't kidding. This is unreal. I still can't believe you can't take this to the authorities." Jack said rubbing his day old stubble.

Sophie looked at Jack and Joe, "I don't know, this has to be the strangest thing I have ever seen. Jack, maybe we should go home, I don't know if I can handle this."

"Hey you're the one who said we love Joe, we are his friends, and we have to help him! You can't back out now.

Joe looked very serious now, "Jack if this is too much, you guys can leave in the morning. I know it is a lot to ask, but we really have it under control. Like I told you we killed about thirty of them. The only problem is, like I said before, we don't know how fast they breed, it is hard to keep up. One of them actually gave birth to five kittens during the hunt, right in front of the camera, just dropped right out, you want to see?"

"No I have seen enough. Let's hit the sack and we will start in the morning. This is starting to excite me now. Come on Sophie. Joe, where are we bunking down at?"

"Just head up the stairs. I have the guest bedroom made up for you. Towels and the rest of the stuff you will need are in the closet by the bathroom. Are you o-k Sophie?"

"Yea, I just need to sleep, it's been a long day."

9

After Jack and Sophie went upstairs Joe went back into command central. He went over all the switches, making sure everything was labeled and in working order. He sat down with a pad of paper and started writing down an outline of all the security measures. Then he pulled out all the radios and put fresh batteries in them. The last thing he needed was to have one of them die out in the field. He placed new head sets with each radio. Quiet was important on a mission like this. Those cats can hear real well, and he didn't want his friends or neighbors getting hurt. The radios would be their life line, the only communication they would have with each other.

Next he opened the gun safe and made sure all the guns had a round of ammo in them, the safeties were engaged and there were a few clips to go with each gun. He went to the closet and pulled out hunting vests for each of them. In the vest were a compass, two flash lights and a switchblade. Josh, Billy, Gavin and Gage had there own hunting attire and hunting knives. In green and black they would be well hidden.

Next he went to the closet to get out the duffel bags; he put two guns and enough ammo in each one to get the job done. These would go up in the deer stands.

Joe went over to the sofa and lay down. His mind was going a mile a minute. 'Why did I get them involved? What am I thinking, this is crazy. But I really need the help.' After beating himself up, Joe drifted off to sleep.

He dreamed, he always dreamed. Ever since the first encounter with those cats, he had been having nightmares. They were always the same.

The cats were chasing him. Joe was always running holding a young cat. It was always screaming. The wild cats would get closer and closer. They would leap in the air, ready to pounce Joe, to destroy him for causing so much pain. Right before they landed on him, Joe would bolt up out of bed. He would be breathing hard and sweating. Most of the time he wouldn't or couldn't go back to sleep.

10

At 4 am, Joe jumped out of bed, something was chasing him again. He had been having bad dreams for the past two weeks. 'Well' he thought, 'I can't go back to sleep now.'

Joe got up and went in to the kitchen. Sophie had cleaned up from dinner the night before and the place never looked so good. The household chores had gotten out of hand. With trying to secure the house and property, and keep safe from those critters, Joe hadn't had much time for cleaning.

The coffee was now brewing, Joe decided to start breakfast. He did have guest didn't he? He got the bacon in the pan and started peeling the potatoes. "A good country breakfast is what I need." He said out loud.

"Talk to yourself much?"

Joe about jumped out of his skin. "What are you doing up this early Sophie? You about scarred me to death!"

"MMM, the coffee smells good. Are you cooking breakfast for me?"

"I thought it would be nice. Bacon, eggs, biscuits and gravy and fried potatoes. How does that sound?"

"Great, I'm starving, can I help?" Sophie went and

poured herself a cup of coffee. "Want some?"

"Sure, lots of sugar, no cream. If you really want to help you can put the biscuits in the oven and turn the bacon, it's about ready. I'll get the potatoes going."

Working in the kitchen took her mind off what might happen tomorrow night. She was anxious to get prepared, learn the security system, and just get organized. Sophie liked to be organized, she liked everything in order.

Jack came walking in to the kitchen, bare feet and in a robe. "Why in gods name are ya'll up so early?"

"Joe is making us breakfast. Here have some coffee. It will help you wake up."

Jack took the cup and sat at the table. He watched Joe and Sophie make breakfast. Jack wasn't much of a morning person.

"I could have slept another couple of hours you know." Jack complained.

"So go back to bed, after I smelled the coffee and the bacon there was no way I could sleep."

"You are always hungry, aren't you?" Jack asked.

"No, just first thing in the morning."

Everyone sat down at the table to eat. The breakfast was good. Joe had become a good cook.

After everyone ate, they helped clean up the dishes.

"Let's get our showers and get dressed. Then I will lay out the plan for tomorrow night and show you how to operate everything." Joe got up and headed for his room.

Jack looked at Sophie, "Are you sure you want to stay and do this? I can tell you, I'm not so sure. I don't want to see anyone get hurt."

"Come on, let's go get dressed and get this day started. Like Joe said, after we see the plan we can leave."

Sophie took Jacks hand and they went upstairs.

11

Everyone met downstairs an hour later. There was tension in the room so thick you could cut it with a knife. For a moment everyone just looked at each other.

Joe stood up. "I guess we should get this show on the road. Let's go to command central first. We can start there."

Jack and Sophie followed Joe to the small office he had set up with computers.

Jack looked around with wide eyes. "Wow! You were busy last night."

There was stuff everywhere, guns, ammo, duffel bags, and flash lights. There were hunting vests, lying on the chair.

"I'm just getting everything ready. You can't be too careful when it comes to guns and crazy critters. Let's start here at the table."

Everyone gathered around and sat down. Joe pointed to the drawing of the house and the property. "I'm going to show you the plan on paper first. Then we will go around and operate everything. Nothing can go wrong."

"Everything is marked the same on paper as it is on the property and in the house. These dotted lines that go from the cellar door out to the property are the tunnels. There are three of them. One goes out to where you guys are parked. One goes up towards Billy's Place. The third one goes up hill about a half of a mile. For each tunnel there are four cameras. There are two in the tunnel at each entrance and two outside the tunnel, one at the house facing towards the end of the tunnel and one at the end of the tunnel facing towards the compound."

"That's a lot of cameras, why don't you have that many monitors?" Jack asked.

"Each monitor is split into four screens. Josh said it was best, it takes up less room in here."

Jack looked over towards the screen, "Those are not very big monitors, and how is the resolution? Can you see everything, especially at night?"

"Gage got the Night vision cameras, it's really cool. Tonight when it gets dark I'll show you.

"O.k. so the cameras will show you guys what is going on inside and outside. The radios are so if anything happens good or bad we can communicate with each other. You have to remember to be very quiet, so I have head sets for each radio so the cats can't hear us.

The only problem with that is if someone is out in the field and needs to talk, they have to make sure the critters are not around."

Sophie picked up one of the radios, turned it on and plugged in and put the headset on. The guys were watching her with interest. There was a 'bright idea' look in her eyes. She pushed a button; no sound was heard because the headset was plugged in. Sophie heard the tone in the head set. "Do you guys have a compass?"

"Sure" Joe answered. "We have them on our hunting vest. Why?"

"I have an idea. If you guys need to know something is coming up on you, Jack or the guys can press a button. You will here a tone and know there is something there, kind of like Morse code. For instance, one beep for north, two for south and so on. It's kind of archaic, but it will cut down on conversation."

"Great idea Sophie, The guys are coming over about four. We will toss around the idea. Let's get back to the map." Joe pointed to the map. "These trees marked with an X, They have spikes and deer stands in them. When we get done here we will go out and I will show you. We are also going to stock them with guns, extra ammo, flashlights and a few other things. That's what these duffel bags are for. If someone gets in a bind out there they can climb up and have a safe area. The cats can probably climb too, but hopefully we will have an advantage, if we can get up there first."

Joe pointed to the house on the diagram. "In the kitchen and in command central there is a bank of switches. They are color coded. Red draws up the stairs, or lets them down. That covers the front door. The green switch operates the metal shutters. They are on all the doors and windows on the outside of the house. The shutters all have peep holes. The blue switch fills the mote with water, and the yellow raises the spikes in the mote. So far we have found out they don't like water, but they still try to jump the mote."

Jack leaned back in his chair. He looked at Sophie then back at Joe. "I guess that is why there is blood on those spikes out there."

Sophie stood up, "I'll be right back, I need some more coffee."

"She looks pale; maybe you should go and check on her"

"She'll be alright. This is all just a little overwhelming." Jack said.

Sophie came back looking a little better, she sat down. "O-k, I'm ready, how do you work these monitors and cameras?"

"There is a main switch that turns them all on, its right here, the black one." Joe flipped on the computers.

"Each monitor has its own keyboard and mouse. There are four cameras to each computer. This is a state of the art system. All you have to do is zoom in on a picture and click the mouse. Double click and it goes back to the split screen."

"This is really cool." Jack sat down in front of one of the monitors and moved the curser, and clicked on of the screen. "Really cool!" he repeated.

Joe stood up and motioned for Jack and Sophie to follow him. They walked out of the room and towards the front door. "I have pistols and Ammo in several places in the house, so no matter where you are you are protected. There are two guns here in the hutch. There is a couple in the drawer under the microwave by the back door. I put two in the drawer in the upstairs bathroom. Let's go to the kitchen."

"So we are set up for warfare," Jack picked up one of the pistols.

"Sophie, I know Jack shoots, do you?"

"Actually, Jack and I went on a date night to a shooting range not to long ago."

Joe looked at Jack, "You're a romantic."

Jack rolled his eyes.

12

It had been several hours since breakfast. While they were in the kitchen, they decided to make lunch. After they all ate and cleaned up they headed towards the front door. Joe stopped and grabbed a duffle bag out of the office. They went outside.

Joe pointed to the cameras on the house and in the trees. All the cameras had a metal cage over them. “That is the position of the cameras, when you watch the monitors you’ll know where the pictures are coming from. Come on, I will show you which trees we have ready.”

Joe, Sophie and Jack hiked about 500 feet down into the woods; he came up on the first tree and climbed the spikes, and opened the duffle. He pulled out an ammo box and two rifles and set then in the deer stand, and then he climbed back down. Jack and Sophie followed him to the other trees and watched as he did the same thing in each tree.

“I have a question.” Sophie said, “If there are three tunnels and only five of you guys, who is going down the tunnel alone? And isn’t that a little dangerous?”

“Well Billy and Josh have been friends for a long time, so they are going together. Gage and Gavin will go up the north tunnel and head down hill towards the compound. I am going to take the tunnel down to the cars by myself and work my way back up."

Sophie laughed, "Just don't go and take a car and leave us up here."

"Don't worry, I am not looking to run from the cats, just destroy them."

"Isn't that dangerous you going alone?" Jack asked.

"Probably, but right now I don't really have a choice. You two need to be inside the house watching the monitors and playing lookout. Everyone else on the mountain is either too young or too old to participate in this little adventure. Half the people who have cabins up here won't even come up till next spring anyway. It just has to be this way. As long as you two watch everything and report back to us everything should be fine. This is a carefully laid plan. Let's go back up to the house and flip a few switches."

"Alright, but I have one more question. Before you put in the cameras, how did you find out so much about these cats, or whatever they are?"

Joe pulled up his sweatshirt. There was a scar from his chest to his belly button. "Experience."

13

Two years ago Joe was living a comfortable life in a small town in Georgia. He drove his Toyota to work everyday to a dealership in Lilburn. He wasn't making much, just enough to live on. He got the call one afternoon on his cell phone while he was showing a car to an older couple. His parent had gotten in a terrible accident in Atlanta. They were on their way to see Joe from their vacation in Florida. After a short visit, they were heading up to Myrtle Beach to visit Joe's sister.

By the time Joe got to the hospital, he found out they had died from their injuries. Joe had to call his sister and brother-in-law and give them the news. Joe's family was always very close, they sometimes went on vacations together, all the holidays were spent together, and it tore Joe up.

Deloris, Joe's sister, came down right away, she was always better at this stuff than Joe was. Thc funeral arrangements were made and a week later the will was read. Their parents had quite a bit of money put away for their retirement. It was split down the middle.

Deloris had to get back home to her family, she had two children and right now the nanny was watching them. They needed their mommy. Joe was supposed to go to back to work but he couldn't. He was just too depressed.

That's when he found the compound. He went to the mountains to get away for a while. The rented cabin was far enough out in the woods but close enough to town. Joe got into town and stocked up on food. He had not been eating much since the funeral, so he figured if he had food in the house he would eat. On a building near the grocery store there was a property for sale board, that's when the compound caught his eye.

The first week at the rented cabin was fine. Joe rested, walked, and fished. He kept thinking about the compound. The price on it was $200.000. He didn't owe anyone any money, except his car and living expenses. His job was just o-k. He really didn't like it much; there was no challenge to selling cars anymore. The lease was almost up on the apartment he was renting, and he didn't have a girlfriend. He had made up his mind.

The compound was his, it needed a lot of work, but he could do most of it himself. The rest he could hire out.

A year and a half later, Joe had still not gone back to work; he was obsessed with the compound, that's when the trouble started.

Every month about the same time, there was damage to the house. Joe would get up and go through his usual routine in the morning. Shower, get dressed, and then have coffee on the porch. He noticed the day after a full moon and new moon. There were scratches on the doors. The window panes were muddy with paw prints, and in the evenings there were a lot of animal noises outside between midnight and daybreak.

Joe already new Billy, they met at the parts store. He was telling him about what was going on, Billy suggested putting up a camera. The next afternoon Billy and Josh came up to the compound to install the camera. The three of them cooked wings on the grill and threw back a couple of beers and generally had a good time, they had been friends ever since.

Just so happens, that night was a full moon.

About eleven PM Billy and Josh went home. Joe was cleaning up the grill and picking up from the little get together. He went in the house to turn on the camera and the computer. He was watching the woods. He thought he saw something, but the camera wasn't positioned just right. Because he thought he had seen something he picked up his hunting knife and attached it to his belt, grabbed the step ladder and headed outside.

As he was repositioning the camera, he heard the noise again. He turned around to see what the noise was. There they were, two of the largest, strangest and meanest looking cats he had ever seen. They were creeping towards him very cautiously. All of the sudden there was a screaming in the woods and one of the cats took off. The other just kept coming towards Joe.

It was moving slow, so Joe decided to slowly come down from the ladder and get into the house. As soon as his feet touched to ground the cat started for him. He opened the door and tried to get into the house. The cats slammed right into the closing door, and knocked Joe backwards. The hunting knife came loose from his pants and went sliding up the hall. As Joe grabbed for the knife the cat grabbed him. Joe knew if he didn't kill the cat the cat was going to kill him.

Then he felt the pain. Claws were digging into him, but he had to reach for the knife. It was his life, he wanted to live. In horrible pain, and watching the cats face come closer to his, he grabbed the knife and plunged it into the cat. The cat was now screaming in pain and anger. Joe had to finish him off. He slid the knife up and down the cat. It finally fell off him in a blooding mess.

Joe just lay there.

He felt blood drip down his side.

He looked down and almost passed out. He was bleeding pretty badly. Joe reached for his cell phone called 911 and then passed out.

He woke up at the hospital, stitched up and sore.

The staff at the hospital wanted all the details when Joe woke up. When they heard the details, they called the police. The Sargent that came out to the hospital wrote his report, and told Joe they would take a look around.

Joe had told him it was all on video, but the Sargent just said they would check into it.

Billy and Josh came up to the hospital and visited. Joe gave the key to the house and had them hire someone to cleanup the mess. And it was a mess. They discussed the camera.

Billy and Josh went up to the house and watched the video feed, they caught the outside portion which was enough to warrant calling the police and the ranger. No one believed it; they thought it was just some wild pack of dogs or maybe a bear. The picture wasn't real clear. They just saw a large animal and it was mad.

The ranger just gave them all the info on keeping food items in the house, cleaning up your grill so the food doesn't attract animals and so on. All of which the men already knew.

So it was time to take matters into their own hands. That's when the house and property became the compound.

Joe, Billy and Josh recruited Gavin and Gage; they were known in town for some pretty wild no fear stuff. They helped the locals and vacationers with an assortment of different problems. Well, the police were not there to help.

They had to come up with a plan to get rid of those cats.

Their plans came together kind of fast. They hired someone to build the tunnels; Billy and Josh installed the security system with all the cameras and computers, and then they had to figure out how to keep those cats out. Joe thought of the mote and that project was started and finished in record time.

They had to get through several months of large cats trying to get in to the compound. It got kind of scary there a few times. That's when the shutters were put up.

14

"Watch out the window."

Jack and Sophie walked over to the window and looked down at the mote. Joe flipped the yellow switch and up came the metal spikes.

Sophie looked surprised, "Wow, Those are very sharp. Where in the world did you get them?"

"Gage knows a metal fabricator, if you look close you will notice they are not only pointed and sharp at the top, they are sharpened like a sword. There is no getting out, once you have landed on one of those blades. Now watch this."

Joe flipped the blue switch. Jack and Sophie watched as the mote started filling up with water.

"Man, you have thought of everything."

"I hope your right," Joe stopped the water "No since wasting water. We will have to fill it up soon enough."

He then flipped the green switch, as the metal shutters slammed into place, Sophie jumped back. The noise was loud. "Sorry, I should have warned you. It's loud and because of that the shutters get closed before sundown. I'm sure the cats are stirring and getting ready to hunt about then, I hear them screaming. I know this is going to sound out there, but, I think they scream when they start growing.

They do it so rapidly it's got to hurt."

"Check out the peep hole in the shutters. Each shutter in the house has them." He flipped the green switch the other way and the shutters opened again.

"Well, you have seen it all, you think you want to stay and help? We could sure use it."

"Sophie, you think we can handle the house, or do you want to head home? It's up to you."

"Thanks a lot, why is it always up to me?" Sophie thought about it a minute, "Lets stay. Can we go for a walk down the tunnel? I want to check it out, and I need to get something from the car."

"The guys will be here in about an hour. We will all do a final walk through and we will go through the tunnel then."

15

In the woods the cats were stirring. They were no longer huddled in their dens, quiet and somber, no longer a soft furry cute little forest animal. It was almost feeding time. They were hungry. They were stretching and yawing, they were growing. Their strange shaped body, no bigger than a house cat, was getting longer and thicker. Their ears were taking on the shape of a wolf. There fur was almost that of a bear.

By midnight, they would be twice their size. By noon the next day, they will have grown four times their size. And by sundown, they would be a large, mean and hungry as a full grown tiger. That's when they start the hunt for food.

Red meat, raw and bloody, that is what they needed to survive another month, till the next full moon. Then it all starts again.

When they start to hunt they will eat anything in their path that moves. They are hungry. Rodents and small animals were first on their list. They need to fill their stomach, expand it. The cats know out of instinct to stretch their bellies, slowly.

For two long nights they will feed. Then their bodies would absorb the nutrients for a month. They live to feast.

16

By 4:45 pm everyone was at the compound. Today was just the walk through. Tomorrow would be the real test. Joe introduced everyone to Jack and Sophie.

"Are we ready for the dry run?" Joe asked.

Billy piped up, "Let's do it!"

The five guys put on their vest, checked the guns, ammo and the hunting knives.

"Lets run through the plan one more time. For today, Jack and Sophie are going to go with me. Tomorrow night they will stay at the compound inside the house and watch the monitors. They are going to be our eyes, and cover our backs." Joe handed everyone their radios and headsets.

Billy turned his on and placed the head set on his head. "Joe, are you still sure you want to go through tunnel one by yourself? That's the most dangerous walk back up the hill."

"If Jack and Sophie don't see anything on the monitors in your areas, they can radio ya'll and you can come my way. Besides I have a bone to pick with these cats." Joe rubbed his belly.

Sophie put her arm around Joe, "You don't have to be a hero. It looks like you have a bunch of friends here to help."

"Don't worry Sophie, We are a team here. Like I said if Billy, Josh, Gavin and Gage don't see anything in their area, they can head towards mine. I am sure I will need the help."

"So, you want us to come down the hill, killing cats if we see them, circle the house and take post in the deer stands?" Gavin asked.

"I think that would work best. The way the cats come towards the house, you guys can pop them from the vantage point."

The five guys geared up. Joe and Jack went into command central and flipped the black switch. The computers came to life. As they walked out the door they flipped the switch for the shutters. The only thing they didn't do was operate the mote, spikes and the water. That could wait till tomorrow night.

Jack asked Joe, "How do we get back into the house if we are all going to go down the tunnel?"

"There is a cellar door in the back, just above the door are emergency switches, they are in a metal box that has a latch. That was a good question, I forgot to tell you that. Then we also have remotes."

The seven of them headed for the cellar door. "Does each team have their remotes for the locks?" Joe asked.

Gavin and Gage held theirs up, "We got ours, and did you change out the batteries?"

"I did, how about you guys, Josh and Billy?"

I have mine and Billy's." Josh handed Billy his remote.

Everyone headed downstairs to the tunnels.

"See you guys in a while," Gavin and Gage headed for tunnel three at the back of the house. They went in and walked up hill through the tunnel.

"Be safe," The others called.

Billy and Josh were going into tunnel two. "We will be watching you from the trees!" They disappeared in to the tunnel.

Jack and Sophie followed Joe in to tunnel one. "Your friends are really nice. They don't talk much, but they are nice."

"They will talk more when they get to know you better, or after a couple of beers, which ever comes first. Anyway they don't agree with me asking ya'll to help with the mission.

I tried to explain that you and Jack, being in the house was the safest position."

"Joe, Sophie and I talked about whether we should stay and help or go home." They was a pause, "We are going to stay and help."

"Alright!" Joe gave them both big bear hugs. "Thank you so much."

"Wait, you didn't let me finish. There is one condition. Nobody gets hurt."

"I promise...On my honor
I will do my best
To do my duty to God
And my country
To obey the scout law
To help other people at all times
To keep myself physically strong
Mentally awake
And morally strong.
That is the Boy Scout promise. And I will abide by it on this mission."

Everyone started laughing as they headed down the tunnel.

17

The tunnel was long and dark. There were lights on, on the way down, but the dirt walls and ceilings swallowed the light. The rich smell of the earth was overwhelming. After a while Sophie got used to it. The smell didn't seem to bother the guys.

It took about 20 minutes to get to the opening at the bottom of the hill.

"That was quick." Sophie stepped out of the tunnel and took a deep breath in. "Jack can I have the keys to the car?"

Handing her the keys he said, "What do need from the car that is so important?"

Sophie unlocked the door, and opened the glove box, "This is what I hope I won't need."

The guys looked stunned.

Joe patted Jack on the back, "Are you packing too?"

"I had no idea...when did you get that? And why didn't you tell me?"

"After our trip to the gun range, I figured why learn to shoot if I don't have a gun. So I applied and bought this one. It's a 'Glock 26'. I went to the range to try it out and it's real nice." She went around to the trunk, opened it and took out a small duffel bag. In it was her holster and ammo. Sophie put on her holster and loaded the gun and checked the safety. She looked like a pro.

Jack watched Sophie. He had a look of admiration on his face, He just couldn't believe it. "Is that all the surprises for now?"

Sophie shook her head and smiled. "What now Joe?"

"Now we head back up to the compound. First, see that camera on that tree?" Joe pointed to the tree. "It faces up towards the compound. When you look at it on the monitor, watch that area over there. We have been watching them, there is a den over there, and we see the cats stirring once in a while."

"That's where I saw the rabbits or cats, whatever they are."

"Yea, the den stays well hidden. I am hoping to stay hidden in the mouth of the tunnel until they leave the den. Then I will follow them up the hill. When the guys get to the end of their tunnel they will wait for you tell them 'all clear,' then they will head towards the compound. The idea is to surround them and blast them."

18

The mutation had begun. They were growing a little faster and little sooner than they were supposed to. The older more mature cats were leaving the den, looking around.

Heads were high in the air, taking in the scents of their surroundings. Some were confused, it wasn't time yet. They were growing and it hurt.

The younger cats were moaning. They were pacing around in the den. Looking outside, they saw their pack wandering, yet staying close.

There was a loud scream. It was a painful scream. A hungry scream. The younger cats ran back inside the den.

The den was a small cave. Blasting from years ago had made the cave. The cats took it over. The number was close to 50 in this one den. Supply and demand had made some of the other cats travel hundreds of miles to start their own family of mutations. They had to eat too. There wasn't enough in this area.

They were changing. Their heads were getting larger, taking on the appearance of a lion. The ears were long and full of hair. There eyes went from brown to an orange gold color. The hour glass shaped body kept its shape for now, when they fed on flesh and blood, it to would expand. Legs and arms were getting longer. The cats were very agile when they were at full size. Until then they were slow, until they consumed some of the energy they needed to hunt big game. Deer were plenty up in the mountains. Sometimes a black bear got in their path, not for long. What they really wanted and craved was in the compound.

Their creator was there, they smelled him. It was time for him to pay for the pain he created.

When Sloan was experimenting with the chemicals and compounding different minerals, there were mistakes. He would kill what he had created, he would dig a hole and dump the compound and body into the hole and bury it. Then he would start over. Of course no one knew what was buried on the property, except the cats. They knew it was there, they smelled it, and the scent drew them to the compound.

19

Sophie jumped, “What was that?”

There was a loud long scream in the distance. Everyone stopped in their tracks. They were half way to the compound.

Joe pulled out his gun and Sophie followed suit. Jack looked at the both of them. “I thought they were not supposed to be out till tomorrow night.”

“There not. They usually don’t start the screaming till tomorrow around noon. We better get to the house.” Joe took out his radio, “Did you guys here that?”

Gage clicked back, “Yes, what the hell are they doing screaming now. You think we are going to get some action tonight?”

Billy clicked in, “We heard it, and we all better get back to the compound. Radio if you have any trouble. We are about at the house now. I’ll go in and check the monitors.”

“You got it. Gage, you and Gavin start heading this way. Billy and Josh are at the house, they are going to keep an eye on the monitors.”

“We are on our way. Hey Joe...”

“Yea?”

“Be careful, those things are mean and fast.”

"I know."

Sophie, Jack and Joe started back up the hill, a little faster now. The screaming stopped, but that didn't mean anything. The cats were unpredictable. Joe handed Jack one of his pistols.

"You think we are going to need this?" Jack checked the safety. He slipped the gun in the pocket of his coat.

"I hope not. But you never know. I'm just glad it's not dark out yet, I didn't bring the night vision goggles."

Up ahead they could see the house. Gage and Gavin were heading that way.

Then there it was another loud scream. There was movement behind them. The radio blasted.

"Watch out behind you!"

It all happened very fast.

At the same time Gavin and Gage started screaming, "Get down, I have a shot!"

Jack grabbed Sophie, and hit the ground. Joe turned to see a giant cat leaping towards him, he dove to the ground, rolling and firing his gun at the same time. The bullet hit the cat but it kept coming, it was screaming.

There was major gun fire coming from behind them. Jack was on top of Sophie, she was screaming for him to get off. There was no way Jack was moving.

The gunfire stopped about the time the dead cat landed on Joe. "Someone help me. This monster is heavy as hell, and he stinks."

Jack got off Sophie, when she sat up; she saw two cats running back into the woods. They didn't go far.

They stopped and turned around and stared at the humans. She stared right back at them, pulled out her gun, flipped the safety, and fired two shots. She hit her mark on one, the other ran off.

Jack ran back over to Sophie, "What the hell do you think you are doing? Are you out of your mind?"

"Hey don't yell at me. This is the point of the mission isn't it? Two down, and who knows how many to go."

Jack just shook his head. Joe congratulated her on her fine marksmanship.

Gage and Gavin ran down to meet them and see if everyone was alright. "We have to get this body over to the woods, it can't be in the path for tomorrow night, and beside we don't need any other animals feeding on it between now and then. Not right here so close to the compound anyway."

It took all four guys to move it far enough into the woods so it wouldn't be a hazard. Sophie followed them with her gun drawn, just in case.

Josh beeped in, "Great work guys. I have it all on tape, and because it's light out it's very clear. The sheriffs' office can't deny this encounter. Come on back to the house, I will put down the stairs and open the door for you."

20

"I think you guys should stay here tonight. I don't know what is going on with the cats coming out in the day light and a day early. What I do know is we are safer in numbers."

Gage said, "I have my stuff here anyway, I'll stay. Check out the video. It's pretty amazing. I think these cats are larger than they were last month."

Billy walked over to the computer monitors and zoomed in on the cats. "Wow, what is going on, I sure wish we had found a journal of the experiments from old Sloan. This is just so hard to wrap my brain around."

"I know the feeling. Our only choice right now is to get rid of them all. Maybe after this is over this month, we can start building lion pits or something." Joe said.

Jack said, "I am sure the park ranger would love to have a bunch of deep holes dug in the woods. It's not very safe for hikers."

Joe stood up, "I'm getting hungry, I am going to go and start dinner. I hope hotdogs are o-k with everyone; it's the only thing I have enough of to feed everyone. Hey Jack, just to be safe, go ahead and engage the security."

"You want to fill the mote?"

"I hate to waste the water, but better safe than sorry. Go ahead. If they decide to come out tonight we'll have to fight them through the peep holes in the shutters."

Everyone went in the kitchen. Joe had a big pot of soup warming on the stove, "This is my mom's chicken soup recipe; I made a double batch about a month ago and put most of it in the freezer."

Sophie opened the refrigerator and started pulling out the ketchup, mustard and cheese for the hot dogs.

"Sounds good to me" Jack said.

Gavin stepped right up to the table and started putting his hot dog together, and then everyone followed. Joe got out bowls and spoons for the soup.

As they ate the conversation turned back to the cats.

Gavin spoke first, "So, what do yall think is going on?"

"As big as those three cats were I saw on the monitor, I think they are just hungry. That's the only thing I can think of." Billy took a bite of his soup.

"Wouldn't it be cool if we had a cage? We could dart one and put it in the cage and have someone from the zoo come and get it and study it." Gage was the youngest of the group, everything was cool to him.

Josh said, "Yea that would be really cool, until it got out. We just don't know how strong these things are. Remember what happened last month?"

Joe looked over to Jack and Sophie, "It was about day break. There were dead cats everywhere. We got about 20 of them; unfortunately we got mostly younger ones. But we got about 8 of the adults. A couple tried jumping over the mote and ended up on the spikes. The sun was coming up and the cats were shrinking before our eyes, they were walking back to the woods. They don't seem to hurt when they are reverting back to there normal size."

"So what happened?" Sophie asked.

Billy spoke up, "We had flipped the switch to turn off the computers, and open up the shutters. We were all in the office; there was a loud crash in the front room. Joe ran in first to find one of those cats hanging half way in the window. When it tried to crash through, the broken glass must have cut an arterie. The cat was bleeding out, and moving real slow, and then it just died. I guess it was a last ditch effort on his part."

Joe walked over to the sink with his bowl and spoon, "It was a real big mess. At least when it is outside we can haul them out to the woods. The other animals and buzzards take care of the rest."

"It took us two days to clean up the blood." Josh was finished with his food and started loading the dishwasher. He was somewhat of a neat freak.

All the dishes were loaded, and the kitchen was cleaned up.

"Come on, let's go in to the livingroom and relax. We are going to need it tomorrow. I guess we will all hit the sack early tonight. So Sophie, what have you been up to these days? We haven't had much time to talk about anything but the crazy cats."

"Well, the design firm is doing well. I just finished a kitchen project on a cute little bungelow. It was built in 1928. Vicky and Ryan are a real nice couple, they were always offering us food and drinks. They pretty much stayed out of the way, which is pretty unusual for homeowners. I did about 5 projects in a row, and I needed a break, that's why we were able to come up for a couple of weeks. Thanks for inviting us.

"Thank's for coming up. I appreciate your help. After Saturday night, we can all relax and enjoy your little vacation. I'll even take you into town. We have some great shops. You will like the antique shops, they are real nice."

"That sounds like fun" Sophie said, "What else is there to do up here?"

"I thought you wanted to come up here and relax?" Jack asked Sophie.

"I do, but relaxing doesn't mean vegging in front of the television the whole time. I want to read and shop, maybe even hike a little, if it's safe."

"I have horses," Billy said. "We can trail ride."

"We usually don't have any problems up here except two nights a month." Joe said.

"Sophie you can ride, horses don't like me." Jack got up, "Hey Joe, you got a beer?"

"Yea, check the fridge."

"Come on Jack, My horses like everyone. There real nice."

"I have gotten thrown, bitten and sneezed at; I am not getting on a horse."

"My, your cranky, let's go lay down, you will feel better in the morning."

"Sorry I snapped at you Billy, I am sure your horses are real nice. I am just a little tired. With the drive up and all the unexpected excitement, I guess I need to hit the sack. Good night everyone."

Jack started up the stairs; Sophie said her goodnights and followed him up.

21

At 2 am the screaming started. Jack and Sophie woke up and jumped out of bed. The screaming was loud. There was banging on the shutters. Sophie got out of bed and started getting dressed.

"What are you doing? They can't get in to the house."

"Well I can't sleep with all the racket going on. Come on, get dressed and come down stairs with me, I'll fix some coffee."

Jack got up and started getting dressed. "O-k, I'm coming"

Jack was always grouchy when he first got up, and today was no different. "I am not going to be any good today if I don't get some rest"

Maybe after the sun comes up you can go take a nap."

"Yea, we will see how that works out. Let's go down, I'm ready."

Jack followed Sophie down to the kitchen. When they got there everyone in the house was up. The coffee was already made. Jack grabbed a cup from the counter and started pouring himself a cup. Sophie put on a teapot of water to boil.

Joe looked tired, "Sorry they woke you."

"Not your fault, it's those damn cats. Why the hell are they out now?"

"I guess they were out yesterday and they are hungry. It's just too early. I'm glad we were smart enough to engage the security system last night. They have been tearing up the shutters. We better go and get the pistols and see what we can take care of now, less to do later."

Everyone got up and went to gather their weapons of choice. Jack, Sophie and Gavin went upstairs. Joe went to the kitchen windows. Billy and Josh went to the front of the house. All of the sudden it was quiet, the cats stopped screaming.

Billy yelled to the others, "I think they left. This is so weird. I don't see anything out the peep holes."

"I am going to the computers and see what they are doing." Joe left the computers and cameras on when he went to bed last night. "Hey ya'll, come here."

Everyone came running to the office. The cats were walking away from the compound.

"Look at that." Gage clicked on the screen of the camera pointing from the house to the woods. "I think we might have a problem."

They were watching two cats in particular. These cats were actually up in the tree stand. One of them was pushing the guns out of the tree stand. After they landed on the ground a couple of other cats were biting and trying to chew up the guns. One of them was carrying a gun off into the woods.

Joe went running from the room, grabbed his 12 gage and flipped the switch to open the shutters. He opened the door and started firing at the cats. Billy and Josh joined him. The cats started running in to the woods.

"I got one." Josh said. "Look the other one is trying to carry it off to the woods"

Then there was gunfire again. Billy had a rifle with a scope. "Got him"

Two giant cats lay at the edge of the woods, dead. Everything was quiet again, dead quiet.

Gage and Gavin came in the livingroom, "All the cats left the compound. This is unreal. If it's this bad now what is going to happen at sundown?" Gavin asked.

"I don't know, but when the sun comes up we are going to have to go out and check the deer stands. We need to see how many guns are gone. Gage, you and Gavin go down stairs and get about 6 rifles and bring them up."

As they went down to the cellar, the others gathered in the office to check out the monitors. On one they saw Gavin and Gage opening up a crate and pulling out guns. The other cameras were still on so they could see what was going on outside. The sun was coming up and it was a little easier to see. They didn't see anymore cats.

"I guess we scarred them away with all the gunfire.' Sophie said. "OH NO, look!"

The camera at the end of the main tunnel showed a cat entering the tunnel.

"Gavin, Gage get up here now, quick! There is a cat running up the tunnel." yelled Joe.

On one screen they watched the cat running up the tunnel, on another Gage and Gavin running up the cellar stairs. Sophie ran to the kitchen cellar door and opened it up for the guys. Jack was right behind her with his gun drawn.

As the door opened, the guys came through; the cat was making his way up the stairs. They slammed the door shut just in time. The cat hit the door with full force. The four of them were leaning on the door. "Joe, Billy, Josh, get in here, NOW!!" Jack yelled.

They came running into the kitchen. Billy and Josh went over to the refrigerator and started pushing it in front of the cellar door. The cat was trying to get through the door.

"What are we going to do?" Sophie asked.

"I don't know right this minute, one problem at a time. If we can't take the tunnels and come up behind them, our plan is pretty much ruined." Joe said.

Billy said, "I am going to go and check out the monitors. Try to see what this cat is doing and see if there are any more."

"Alright, I think this is all we can do for now, this ought to hold him out. If I could get out to the shed and grab some supplies I can barracade this door. Damn, this sucks all this hard work. How did they get so smart?" Joe looked pissed off.

Billy yelled out to the others, "There aren't any more in any of the tunnels. I am checking the outside cameras. Joe, you need to come in here and see this."

"Crap, what now?" Joe went running in to the office. "What's going on Billy?"

The others followed Joe into the office.

"We have big problems, check this out."

Joe looked at the computer screen, leaned over to

the bank of switches and engaged all the switches. The others watched the screen, the mote was filling up with water, and the spikes came up. The shutters were slamming against the house.

"The cats are coming back toward the compound, there are about twenty of them. They are walking very slowly, this is strange." Billy said.

Jack spoke up, "Look the cat in the cellar is leaving." They watched the cat go back out the way he came.

The other cats stopped right before the mote. In unison they let out a scream so loud, the birds went flying from the trees.

"Look" said Sophie, "They all leaving"

"This is so strange" Josh said. "It must be that the sun is coming up. I don't think they like the sun. It looks like we are going to have to work fast."

"Yea, we never see them during the day when they are this large" Gavin said. "I have seen them in the woods like the rest of you when they are small and docile."

Billy looked over to Joe, "So what do you think we should do?"

22

The cats were going back to their dens. It wasn't just luck the one cats found the opening to the tunnel. Even in their small state they were watching. The humans just thought they were dumb forest animals. They were smart, the man made them smart. The man made them hurt. The man also made them hungry.

Now it was time to rest, and to grow.

In just 18 hours the hunt would begin.

They would find the man, and destroy him.

They would feast, and grow.

23

Joe took Billy and Josh with him, the others were going to stay in the office and watch the monitors, just in case the cats decided to come back. In the kitchen they moved the refrigerator. Josh opened the door.

"My god, look at what that cat did to the door, we are going to have to reinforce it before tonight."

"Man, he destroyed it. Josh said.

The three of them walked down the stairs, the place was trashed. The crates with the guns in them were tore apart. There were boxes of ammo spilled out on the floor; some of the guns were lying on the floor.

"I think we should get most of the guns and ammo upstairs." Joe said. "When we get this done, we can go out to the shed and bring in some wood and fix the door."

"You got it." Billy radioed upstairs, "Everything clear outside? Are those cats still gone?"

"No sight of them, all's clear." Gavin said.

"Alright, we are coming up with the guns and ammo." Billy said.

Gage, can you and Gavin sort out the ammo and check the guns, we need to go out back and grab some things to fix the door?" Joe asked.

"Sure, make sure you guys put on your vests, and

bring your guns and radios." Gage advised.

Jack asked, "You guys need an extra hand? I kinda feel useless."

"Sure, come on." Joe said, 'Sophie you mind fixing some food, its only 6am but I feel like I have been up all night."

"You have," Sophie said, "Of course, I will get breakfast going."

Jack helped Joe, Billy and Josh gather the wood, nails, hammers and an electric saw and carry it back to the house. He was relieved there was no more excitement for now. Jack felt like they were being watched. And they were.

When they got back to the house, Billy pressed the remote to let them in, and then flipped the switch to draw the shutters again. The four of them went into the house. Billy and Joe dropped the wood on the kitchen floor. Josh put the nails and hammer on the table. Jack had the saw; he put it on the counter.

"What ya making there Sophie?" Jack asked.

"Breakfast, what does it look like?"

"Hey, don't bite my head off." Jack said.

"I'm sorry; I am just tired and hungry. You know I usually eat as soon as I get up. It's been three or four hours and I am starving, and I have a headache."

"Here let me help you"

Jack brought Sophie some Advil, and started helping her in the kitchen. He took over making the sausage, while Sophie was making pancakes. The kitchen was coming alive in activity.

The guys were measuring and cutting wood to reinforse the door, then came all the hammering.

Sophie was glad she took the pain reliever.

"I think I'm going to install these two brackets on either side of the cellar door. This plank of wood can sit on the brackets and fortify the door, just in case."Joe said.

"Good idea," Sophie said. "I don't want one of those things to get in here, especially while eveyone is gone."

"I'll be here to protect you honey." Jack said

Sophie leaned over and gave Jack a kiss. "Thanks Jack."

The door was getting done, breakfast was cooking, and everyone was busy. The hour was 7am.

"Come on ya'll come and get it. Breakfast is served." Sophie hollared.

24

Joe and Billy reinforced the door the cat destroyed. There was no way anything was going to get into that door again.

Everyone was done with breakfast; Sophie cleaned up the breakfast dishes. The guys sat around and talked.

"So what is the plan for tonight?" Josh asked.

"I vote we keep the same plan, unless something else happens before sunset." Gage said.

"I agree, we will watch the monitors throughout the day and see what happens." Joe said.

Josh got up and poured himself another cup of coffee, "What if they get into the tunnel again? Tunnel one is the most important tunnel, it puts you behind them."

Jack stood up pacing in the kitchen, "I know we are just here to watch and help out, but, I think someone needs to go into the tunnel with Joe. If those things are coming up the tunnel while Joe is going down, it could mean disaster."

"There is no one else to go with me. Besides, that would leave only one person behind in the house. It could only be Sophie, and I won't let that happen.

Sophie spoke up, "I don't know why, the doors and

windows are secure. I would have a radio, and the computers. If I see anything going on I can radio you guys and someone can rescue me. Gage and Gavin would be the closest. Tunnel three is also the shortest to the compound."

"No." said Jack, "You are not going to be alone in this house, with those things out there."

"Why not? You have seen me shoot. You know I am capable of hitting my target. Is it because I am a woman?"

"No, it is because you are my woman."

"Look, you two stop this, let me think." Joe said as he was rubbing his head.

"Joe, we have never seen any cats going up hill. They are always coming towards the compound. They are obviously smarter than we thought. They know about tunnel one. Why don't I go with you, Gage goes alone in tunnel one. It's a short tunnel, and a short hike back to the compound." Gavin stopped to see what Joe's reaction was.

"No, this is my fight. For some reason they are after me and this place."

Sophie cut in, "Are you sure you didn't find anything anywhere in this place to give you a clue what this is all about?"

"Look, I told you, I had a dumpster brought out here, and cleared the place out. It was before all this started, so I didn't know anything was important."

"Show me where the lab was."

"Sophie, this is a waste of time. It's now 8am and we have a lot to do."

"Like what?" Sophie asked Joe.

"Like everything, we need to get outside and recheck the deer stands; we need to make sure everything is in working order. What if we have another daytime encounter with the cats? We need to be watching and ready."

Billy stood up, "Hey, Joe, calm down, it's only eight o clock. We have plenty of time. We are a team; we will get it all done."

"I have an idea," Sophie said. "Let Gavin and Gage go and check the deer stands, Billy and Josh can check out the rest of the security measures. I want to go downstairs and check out the area you said was a lab. It shouldn't take long. Joe, you and Jack can come with me. You guys can protect me."

Joe stood up, "Alright, Just for an hour. There really isn't much to see."

Billy and Josh went to the office to check out the controls for the shutters and the mote. The computers were still on.

Gavin and Gage followed Jack, Joe and Sophie down the stairs. They needed to gather up more guns and ammo to replace the ones in the deer stands if needed. Everything had to be rechecked. After the last experience with the cats they didn't know what to expect. Joe, Jack and Sophie walked to the back of the cellar. There was a door just past the washer and dryer. It was blocked with boxes.

"What's in all these boxes?" Sophie asked.

"Just a bunch of Mom's and dads stuff I couldn't part with. The usual stuff, dishes, dust collectors and other stuff. Deloris and I split up everything we wanted; the rest went to Good Will. Come on and help me move these boxes and we will check out the lab, or what ever you want to call it."

They moved the boxes and stacked them up on the adjacent wall. There were about 20 of them and they were heavy. About 20 minutes later they opened the door. Joe reached in and turned on the lights.

It was large room, about 20 x 20. There were fluorescent lights hanging on chains, it was very bright. Across the middle of the room there were work benches. Under each bench there were drawers and cabinets. On the walls, there were shelves. The only other thing in the room was four doors. All the benches and shelves were empty.

"What's in the closets?' Jack asked as he went towards one of the doors.

"They are just closets with shelves instead of clothes hangers. There were all sorts of test tubes, and other lab stuff. Like I told you, I trashed everything."

Sophie walked over to where Jack was standing, Jack opened the first closet. Joe wasn't lying, there were only shelves in the closet. Leaving the door open, they opened each closet and looked in.

In the last closet, on the shelves, there were stacks of material.

"What's all that material for?" Sophie asked.

"I don't know, it was here when I moved in. I figured I would keep it and use it for curtains or something. I forgot about it until you opened the door."

Sophie went over to the material and pulled out some of the folded pieces. "I wonder what he was using it for. Did you take the material out of other closets and put it all in this one?"

"No, it was already folded nice and stacked up, so I just left it."

"Do you mind if I take it out and lay it on the table?" As she asked the question, Sophie removed the material from the closet.

"Be my guest. Why?" Joe started walking towards the closet.

"I am just curious. Why would an old man that proclaims to be a scientist have folded material in a lab closet? I wonder if he was trying to hide something."

Jack spoke up, "What are you thinking Sophie. That mind of yours is always in motion. You're like a private investigator rather than an interior decorator."

"I am an Interior designer, not a decorator"

"What's the difference?" Joe asked

"I design rooms, and have other people decorate. Really, it's just a play on words."

"Yea, o-k." Joe said

Sophie was pulling the material out of the closet when something fell out of one of the pieces of fabric. She bent down and picked up what appeared to be a journal. Joe and Jack walked towards her to see what she picked up.

"Well well, what do we have here?" Sophie asked. "Looks like a journal of some sort."

"Out of all the stuff I tossed out, there was nothing in writing. Just lab equipment and most of it was trashed, or burned in some way. Open it up, what does it say?" Now Joe was interested.

"Hey guys, look over here." Joe and Sophie walked back over to the closet door. Jack pointed towards the back of the closet. "Wonder what is behind the wall. Looks like someone cut out a door in the back of the closet."

The guys started to pull out the shelves. Sophie put

the journal down on the bench and helped Joe and Jack pull the shelves out of the closet.

They turned to see who was coming down the stairs. It was Billy.

"I thought you guys got lost down here. I have been watching the computers and all is good outside, so far. Josh is hanging out in the office, so I could check on you guys. What is all this?"

"I wanted to check out the lab and look what I found." Sophie was pointing to the journal. "Jack also found something else a little interesting."

Billy walked over to the closet and looked in.

"I'm going to need a few tools, I'll be right back." Joe left the lab and went to the cellar. A few minutes later he came back with the tool box.

"What do you think is hidden behind the wall?" Billy asked.

"I don't know, but I am going to find out. Maybe we will find something to help us get rid of the cats."

While Joe and Billy were trying to pry the fake wall away from the molding, Sophie went back to the journal and opened it up about mid way. She started reading, and then gasped.

"Oh no, listen to this." The guys stopped and turned to Sophie. She started reading from the journal.

'I'm glad my mind is going; now I will not have to live with the evils that I have created.

I am sure the bodies will not be found on the property, they will decompose under the ground. I will need to dispose of all data and parts before I go. I must not let the cancer take me before the job is complete. I have much work to do...'

"Whoa, I wonder what that is all about." Sophie said. "It sounds like he was trying to hide something.

Joe did you find any parts, when you cleaned out the lab?"

"Nothing, The bottles and jars were all empty. The equipment looked ancient and it was pretty trashed down here. Like someone went crazy and trashed it on purpose."

Jack looked at Sophie, "Why don't you go upstairs and read that journal while we try to pull down this fake wall."

"Great idea, I'm a bit chilled, I'll go up and make some hot tea and read."

Sophie started up the stairs. The guys continued tearing out the fake wall in the closet.

25

Sophie put water in the teapot to boil. She took out the teabags and the sugar. She grabbed the coffee cups from the counter. The guys would probably like something hot; it was cold in the cellar.

There was a lot of noise coming up from the cellar. Sophie sat down to read the journal where she left off.

'The experiments didn't do so well. These cats have started to grow on the full moon. I don't know what went wrong with the formula. They were supposed to get smaller. The idea was to make a sweet furry miniature pets. This was my chance to really show the town people I could do something.'

Flipping through the book, Sophie read from another page.

'I have had to destroy four cats this week. They have become aggressive to the touch. They scream and moan when I come around them. The pit in the back is starting to smell. I need to get out there and cover them with lime and dirt.'

"There is nothing in this book about how his experiments were done." Sophie spoke out loud.

Sophie kept flipping through the pages, she noticed there was only complaining about what went wrong and destroying the animals.

'Tonight I will start a bonfire, it's going to rain, and it's a good time. The burn permit will keep away the fire department. I need to get rid of the proof of what I have been doing.'

Sophie thought, "This guy was nuts. All he cared about was his own rear end. What about the people who live up here? These cats are clearly dangerous."

Sophie got up to pour herself a cup of tea. She went to the steps and opened the door. "Hey, are ya'll doing o-k down there?"

Jack yelled up the stairs, "Yea, we are done tearing out the wall, come down and check it out."

Sophie put her cup down and started towards the stairs. There was the smell of formaldehyde coming up into the house.

"What is that awful smell?" Sophie asked.

"It looks like to me, our good doctor, or what ever he claimed to be, liked saving body parts." Joe said.

"That's disgusting! Why would anyone want to save eyes and organs?" Sophie asked.

"Did you find out anything in that journal?" Jack asked.

"No. Looks like all he wrote down was his thoughts about getting rid of the problem. He knew he messed up, and was trying to figure out how to dispose of the dead animals. I haven't read the whole thing; I was just flipping around, trying to find something important."

Jack went over to one of the shelves in the little room beyond the wall. There was a black metal box sitting on the shelf. The box had a lock on it.

"It looks like Dr. Jeckel was trying to hide

something." Jack pulled out the box and set it on the work bench. "This lock can be opened with a safety pin. All this doesn't make since."

Joe left the lab and came back a few seconds later with bolt cutters and cut the lock off the box. He opened the box to find a single sheet of paper.

"What the...well let's see what this tells us." He started reading the piece of paper. "It's a list of words. This is really weird. Anyone here into biology?"

"What is on the list?" Jack asked.

"Here it is Biology, Hybrid, crossbred, meiosis, Chromosome levels, sexual reproduction, eukaryotes, and binary fission. The list goes on. Does anyone have a clue?"

"Looks to me like the guy was some sort of biologist or zoologist or something. He was obviously doing some sort of experiments on what ever is out there." Billy said.

"I can take the list up to the computer and do a search on those words and then we can see if we can figure out what he was doing. I'm no scientist, but I am good on the computer." Sophie took the list from Joe.

"Look it is getting to be about 11 o'clock and I am getting hungry. Let's go see how Gavin and Gage did outside and check out the monitors. I am sure Josh is getting tired of sitting in front of the computers for the last several hours." Joe walked out of the lab and the others followed.

"I think we should lock the door to the lab." Billy said.

"You are probably right. What if those cats are trying to get something in here?" Joe said.

Jack looked at Joe, "You aren't serious, and they

are animals. They aren't smart enough to know they were created here."

"They were smart enough to destroy those guns and make their way up the tunnel to the cellar door. Don't underestimate them. I know this is all a little crazy, but I would rather be safe than sorry." Joe said.

26

Everyone had come upstairs and into the office. Sophie was hitting keys on the computer, and writing down the definition of the words found on the list. Josh got up and went to the restroom. Billy sat down in his place at the monitors. Gage and Gavin came into the office, they looked cold.

"Man, the wind is really picking up out there. Those cats only got to one deer stand; we cleaned up the mess and replaced the guns and ammo. Those rifles are trash." Gage said.

"Yea, they chewed them to bits. The ammo was left alone, but they chewed up all the wood on the guns. It's strange, the metal was mangled." Gavin added.

"By the looks of today's events, these cats are strong and growing stronger. I am going to call the sheriffs office and see if we can get some help up here." Joe said.

"Do you really think they are going to help?" Jack said.

Josh came back into the room, "Let me call down to Sergeant Callahan. I have known him for years now. We used to hunt together."

"I didn't know you hunted." said Billy.

"I don't anymore. I used to though. Now the thought

of hunting down innocent animals for food or fun seems slightly wrong to me."

"Thank you." Sophie said. "I have some of the words looked up, get this. The word "meiosis" comes from the Greek verb meino, which means "To make small" Isn't that interesting. The cats grow larger but he was interested in making them smaller. In his journal, it said he wanted to crossbreed two nice animals to make one, but he wanted it to be a tiny version. He wanted to make his mark by selling this new pet to people."

"So you think he did the opposite, and made them grow larger and vicious? Jack asked.

"Well, all these words lead to reproduction, and DNA. So he obviously wasn't a smart scientist, because he messed up big time. We will probably never know what he was doing down there. It says in the journal he had to keep killing the animals and burying them on the property. That is probably why the cats keep coming back here. They smell there own kind."

"You're right; they do keep coming back here. No one else on the mountain has really had a run in with the cats but me. Josh call Callahan, See if he can get up here before sundown, preferably with reinforcements."

"I'm on it now." Josh left the office and went to the kitchen where it was quieter. He picked up the phone, there was no dial tone. He dropped the phone and ran back into the office. "I think we have a problem, the phone is dead. Joe let me use your cell. Mine is charging for tonight."

"What do you mean the phone is dead?" Joe lifted

the receiver in the office, it too was dead. "Josh did you see anything on the monitors while we were downstairs."

"No, I didn't see a thing." Josh dialed the sheriff's number and waited for the connection. "It may have happened this morning while we were fighting off that cat."

Joe looked at Jack, "So you think these cats aren't smart? I think they are trying to hunt us down while we are trying to hunt them down."

"You may be right." Jack said.

Josh was connected to the police station, "May I speak to Sergeant Callahan?" He asked. Josh waited till Callahan picked up the line. "Callahan, its Josh Carter... Yea how ya doing? Listen, can you and a couple of your officers come up to Joes? Yes now... We have a big problem up here and need your help... Yes it's about the cats...No, but listen, we have proof, and if we don't get some help someone is going to get hurt...Alright, see you in a couple of hours, but listen, they are going to come out at dark if not before. So be prepared. Bye."

"Sounds like he didn't believe a word you said." Joe said.

"He didn't. This really pisses me off. Here we are with video proof, animal parts, journals and who knows what else. And he was giving me a hard time."

"Let's get some lunch and figure out what else we can do, if they don't show up, we proceed with our plan. We have got to get rid of these cats." Joe slammed his fist down on the desk and left the room.

27

Everyone went into the kitchen. Leftover soup and sandwich makings were taken out of the refrigerator. There was a quiet among them, everyone was in deep thought. There was a lot to think about. Hybrid cats, body parts, a crazy doctor, and those vicious cats that will be out tonight. Cats so crazy and hungry, they will rip through anything to get at human flesh. Animals so insane, yet smart they know what the plan is. The team sat in still silence, consumed in thoughts of how the plan was going to work, or not work.

Joe was toying with his sandwich. Jack was tapping his spoon on his bowl of soup. They all looked so damned depressed. Sophie got up from the table first.

"Alright ya'll, snap out of it, it already feels like the "Twilight Zone" around here."

"Your right Sophie, I need to get up and figure this thing out, it's still early. We have work to do."

"What else can we do?" Josh asked.

"I think we should build a barricade in tunnel one, a door so that if the cats come back up the tunnel they can't get into the cellar."

"Good idea, do we have enough materials?" Billy asked.

"I think so; we can use the door to the lab. Between

the six of us, we can get the door down and put it up at the base of the tunnel. Sophie can watch the monitors."

"I think that will work. We will bring the radios down stairs that way if Sophie sees anything she can radio us. Do we have extra batteries?" Gage got up from the table and stretched.

"Yes, I put extras in the vests." Joe said.

Gavin got up and put his trash in the can, "Let's get the ball rolling. We never know what is going to happen next."

"Sophie, listen for the door, maybe Callahan will show up. I have a feeling we are not top priority." Joe said.

"I will, I will be able to see anyone coming up in front of the house anyway." Sophie left the room and went into the office.

The rest of the guys cleaned up their lunch plates and headed downstairs. Joe turned on his radio and pushed the talk button, "Sophie, you read me, out?"

"Loud and clear. I will see ya'll in a bit. Be careful. Out."

28

The cats were growing rapidly now. Creeping in the woods surrounding the den, the cats moved around in stealth like manor. Still, they could not stop stretching their limbs; it hurt to move around as they grew. They were now four times the size they were this morning when the sun came up. The younger of the pack were moaning and growling, their stomachs needed food. There had been very little food for a month. They knew it was time to hunt, to eat, and to kill.

A large male sauntered out of the dense underbrush of the woods and joined the pack. For some reason he had reached his full size too early. He was hungry, but he had work to do. Getting the pack ready for sundown was his job; he somehow knew what he had to do. They had to be strong.

Images flashed in his mind. The man, the lab, the smells, and the pain, that is what he remembered. He was one of the first. The others had been born from the original few, and now they are gone. The man had killed his mates. The man will pay.

He strutted around, upright and proud. The cat was checking the pack. He went to each cat, smelled them, licked them and moved to the next, like they were his harem. He would protect them tonight. They knew by instinct what to do. The compound is where they would find what they needed to survive another month.

After he checked everyone, he disappeared back into the woods. It was time to hunt small game, get food back to the pack, instinct took over, he had to make the others strong, and it was almost time. Once the pack received a small amount of nutrition they could hunt on there own.

A small rabbit came out of the brush. The male breathed in the air, his stomach rumbling from hunger. He went to the rabbit; it lay still in front of the cat, trembling. He just smelled the small creature, he could not eat this animal, this was his beginning. The male stepped back a couple of steps and the frightened rabbit hopped off into the brush. As the cat was walking off, the scent of something larger was in the air.

A huge buck was grazing in a grassy sunlit area of the woods, he heard a noise His ears perked and twitched. Head held high now, he looked around. He too caught a scent, and took off. He could sense the chase and hear the pounding feet on the hard earth. The male was after him. As the buck ran faster, the male slowed down, he was too weak, smaller game was what he needed.

After an hour of hunting, the male brought a wide assortment of his kill to the den. Squirrels, raccoons, and possums were the nutrition they needed. The pack was hungry; he left them the food and was gone again for more.

29

While the men were working on building the door in the cellar, Sophie was in the office on the computer watching the monitors. She checked to see if the computers were recording what ever was going on outside. She checked out the feed from each camera, zooming in and out, trying to get a good look in the daylight of anything that may be important. Deciding there was nothing interesting going on outside, she reached for the journal. She opened it up and started to read.

'I have checked and rechecked all the formulas. I swear I am not missing anything. I find it strange the cats grow larger during the full moon. They have gotten larger and meaner each month. The house has been broken into four times now. It is time to go into town and get more ammo and food. I must repair the doors before next week, for it is a full moon again. These animals must be destroyed.'

Sophie flipped to another page.

'My days are becoming longer and harder. The doctors in town say my cancer is spreading. I must finish off these creatures. I must start packing.'

She flipped to the last page of the journal.

'Today I am leaving this hell I have created. The

property is sold and my life is about over. I will move into a nice nursing home until my demise. I pray the young man who lives here will be a good omen and the cats will retreat into the mountains and never return. If not, God help him.'

Sophie sat back in the hard chair and stared at the monitors, she wasn't really seeing the screens. She was in deep thought. How could a man do this and not keep a record of what he did? What if the experiments were written down and they were long gone. Joe had cleaned out the lab and trashed everything. He also said the lab was destroyed, like someone or something went crazy and turned the place upside down.

Something on one of the screens caught her eye. Sophie turned her attention to the computer. There was a cat pacing in front of the tunnel one entrance.

"Hey Jack or Joe, anyone hear me?"

"Go ahead Soph... This is Jack I hear you loud and clear."

"There is a large cat pacing in front of the tunnel."

"We here you, and the door is almost complete. Let us know if he starts up the tunnel."

"You got it; my eyes are on the screens."

Sophie watched the cat; the cat was watching the woods. All of the sudden the cat jumped on top of Jacks car. He looked straight into the camera. Sophie jumped back; she looked straight into the cats eyes. There was an evil in his eyes.

"Jack? This cat is on top of your car, starring straight into the camera. It's like he can see me."

"Damn, on top of my car? I'll be right up"

A few moments later the cellar door opened, Jack

and Gavin came into the office. They looked at the computer screens; the cat was still just sitting there.

"I wonder just what is going through his mind. How smart are they?" Gavin asked.

30

Everyone came up from the cellar and went into the office. Jack and Gavin were watching this cat sitting the car.

"We had better come up with a better plan, it's getting late and I want to be ready for the worst." Gage said.

"Sophie, I guess we haven't heard from the sherrif's office, have we?" Josh asked.

"No and I have not seen anything on the monitor except that cat."

About that moment the cat jumped off the car and went into the woods.

"Well, I guess he got tired of stairing at us." Josh said.

"Look, we never see the cats in tunnel three or up on the hill. Let's barricade the tunnel and team up so there is more coverage here." Billy suggested.

"I agree with Billy. We really need to kill as many of these things as we can. They are breeding faster than we can get rid of them." Gavin said.

"You know there is something we haven't done yet." Josh said.

"What are you thing about now. We only have about three hours before sundown. That's not much time." Joe said.

"We should set out those live traps you have in the attic."

"Josh, those are for small animals, you know these cats are large."

"Listen to my idea. The cats want something here. It may be just the scent of there own buried here, it may be something else. Let's put a few items in each trap including poison."

"O-k, that sounds good. Where are we going to get poison this late in the game?" Joe asked.

"Do you have any antifreeze, in the garage?" Gavin asked.

"Oh yea, antifreeze is sweet, animals are drawn to it and like the taste. I have about a gallon left. I wonder if we should put a few of those jars in and maybe some of that material in the traps with a bowl of antifreeze." Joe was on a roll. He got up and started towards the garage.

Joe brought in the antifreeze and set it on the kitchen table. He then went into the hall and grabbed the pull cord for the attic stairs. Up the stairs he rose and a few minutes later he called down to the others.

"Hey Josh, Jack, anyone, I need some help here."

The guys went into the hall; Joe handed down five traps to them and climbed down. They took the traps into the kitchen.

"Let's go back down stairs and get a few things from the lab." Joe said.

They went down to the lab and gathered material and jars of body parts and brought them back up the stairs. In the kitchen Sophie pulled out glass bowls to fill with the antifreeze.

"Let's put a piece of material on the bottom of the

cage and then when we get outside partially cover the cages." Sophie suggested.

Everyone started outside.

"Wait a minute, we are not thinking. Someone needs to stay inside and watch the computers. We need our radios and vest. Our guns might come in handy." Joe said.

"Sophie, you stay inside and we will get this done and be back shortly." Jack ordered.

"Wait a minute, why do I always have to be the one to stay behind. You guys are such chauvinist. Let me go out this time, I am already going to be stuck in the house tonight."

"O-k Ms.Rambo, I'll stay in and you go out. It doesn't bother me."

Jack went to the office and got her gun and clips and brought them to her. The men and Sophie put on a vest. Everything was checked as if they were going into battle. The guys grabbed the traps and jars. Sophie held the material, the antifreeze and the bowls. Off they went, to the outdoors to set some traps they hoped the cats would get into.

During the next hour the six of them treked through the woods. They set up six traps spread out just beyond the property line. They had spaced them about 300 feet apart. Each trap had a bowl of antifreeze in it. A layer of the material they had found and a jar of some organ was also placed in the trap. To finish it off, Sophie laid a piece of material on top of the cage and propped the door open. The goal was not to trap the cats, but to get them to drink the antifreeze, which was poisonous. If the cats were sick they might be slowing down and Joe and the guys would have a chance to kill the cats before the cats attacked them. Also the ones they didn't get may just die from the poison.

Joe gathered up all the extra stuff and put it in the duffle bags. The others joined him and they started back towards the compound.

As they started back up the hill they heard the screams. The cats were out and roaming they smelled the humans.

In an instant, guns were drawn; the six of them were in a circle facing out towards the woods.

"That was a little scary." Said Sophie.

"Yea, they do that all night while they are out hunting and trying to get into the compound." Gage said.

"I think I am glad I will be in the house, just don't tell Jack." Sophie laughed nervously.

Everyone laughed, and the circle broke. There was no sight of the cats.

"Lets get back; we have a few more things to do to get ready." Joe said.

31

In two hours it would be dusk, the cats would start their way to the compound, ready to feast.

Reaching full size and strength was a painful undertaking for the cats. The older of the pack had hunted small game all day and fed their young. Then they fed themselves. They were ready. By instinct they knew it was not safe to go too far out into the woods during daylight. It was coming. Feeling it in their bones they were ready, kill the man. Punish him for the pain. Feast.

32

"Well folks, we have about an hour before the sun starts to set. Gage, would you flip the switch for the mote, the water and the blades?" Joe asked.

"Sure thing boss." Gage said, "Do you think it will fill in time?"

"It should, we may not see anything till midnight, but you never know."

"Those cats are already stirring, we have seen that. Maybe we should go ahead and get down in the tunnels." Gavin suggested.

Jack looked at Joe, "Joe, I really think someone should go with you."

"I am beginning to think you are right." Joe stood up. "Gavin, How about you go alone in tunnel three. Get back here fast and help Sophie. Billy and Josh will still go in tunnel two, and Jack and I will go in Tunnel one. Sophie do you mind staying here alone for a couple of hours?"

Sophie stood up "No, I don't mind. As long as the cats can't get in, I think I can monitor the computers and keep everyone posted."

"Are you sure you want to do this Sophie?" Jack asked.

"Sure, Gavin should be back here in no time, and

then if anything happens he will be here to help me."

"Hey, what about me?' Gage asked.

"You my friend, I want you to go and climb up in one of the deer stands and do what you do best. Kill something, kill a lot of something."

"Alright, then it is settled, we leave in one hour."

Sophie got up and grabbed the journal off the table. "I'm going to go in the kitchen and make some coffee and read a little. This crazy man, Sloan, had to write something we can use."

Joe turned to the computers and set them so that the screen saver would not come up. He then engaged the shutters. There was a loud bang when they came down. On the monitors there was no sight of the cats.

"Alright guys recheck everything in your vests. I'm going to go and get some of that coffee, it smells good."

Billy and Josh followed Joe into the kitchen. Joe got the coffee mugs off the counter and poured himself a cup. Billy poured Josh and himself a cup and sat down.

"Did you find anything yet?" Billy asked Sophie.

"Not much, lots of complaints about how everything went wrong. It seems this guy Sloan was a bit nuts. He was a self proclaimed scientist."

"Don't you have to have some sort of an education before you know what to do in any type of experimenting? And where would he get the drugs?"

"Who knows, I don't know much about this guy. Just what I am reading. He doesn't sound to educated by the way he writes."

"Hmmm, Like Joe said the good stuff could have been thrown away a year ago." Billy said.

Sophie sipped her coffee and read a little more.

Billy and Josh sat at the table and checked out the things in their vests, and talked. Joe took his coffee back to the office where Gavin and Gage were.

"You guys ready for this?" Joe asked

"Never been more ready." Gavin said.

"You know I really appreciate your help in this, I pray that no one gets hurt. Have you seen the sheriff yet?"

Gavin said, "No, everything on the monitors is clear."

"I just don't get it. We have proof, we have video, and sound. We have body parts for god's sake. We even have a journal. Why won't they believe us?" Joe slammed down his fist on the desk.

"I don't know Joe, but when this is done this time and all the bodies are slacked up, I am going to personally go to the FBI and the newspaper..."

Joe cut him off. "What did you just say?"

"I said I was going to go to the FBI and the newspaper."

"The newspaper, why didn't I think of that?" Joe was pacing the room.

Joe picked up his cell phone. Then he put it down. "It's too late."

"What do you mean, it is perfect. You call the paper, they sent their people up here, they might even send helicopters... Oh yea that would be bad right now."

"All the commotion might send the cats back to their den or even worse they may leave this area and terrorize other people." Joe said "Damn, I guess we call them tomorrow. The ones we don't get tonight will be out tomorrow night." Joe sat back down at the computer.

"If we call them first thing in the morning, and

explain everything they could come out and set up quietly.” Gage said.

“Good idea, if we get through tonight we will do that.” Joe said.

“I guess we should be going.” Joe called everyone into the office.

33

The sun was setting. As the minutes passed it was getting darker. Joe and the guys geared up and headed down to the cellar. It was a mess from the construction of the new door.

Joe radioed Sophie. "Hey, Sophie, you read me?"

"Loud and clear." Sophie came back. "Everything looks good in the tunnels, and there is no activity outside yet."

"O-k we are out into the wild. Let us know if you see anything."

Joe and Jack went into tunnel one. They closed and barricaded the door and started down the tunnel.

Billy and Josh headed for tunnel two. It leads up towards Billy's house. About half way, the tunnel came out near a bunch of boulders and trees.

Gavin entered tunnel three by himself. The tunnel went uphill a quarter of a mile. It would take him a little longer than normal because some of the tunnel was short, and Gavin would have to stoop down to get through.

"I'm in the tunnel and heading up the hill." Gavin radioed to the others.

"Were doing good too." Billy said into his radio.

"So are we, but there is a bad smell here in tunnel

one. I will let you know if we see anything." Jack said.

"I'm here in the nice warm house watching you guys, and all is still clear."

It didn't take to long to walk the length of the tunnel. The guys were taking it slow just in case something decided to enter the tunnel from the other end and head their way.

A half hour later Gavin made it to the end of his tunnel. He got out with his gun drawn and stretched. A deep breath of the cold night air felt good in his lungs. Gavin readjusted his clothing and checked his vest to make sure everything was in tact. He then radioed in to Sophie.

"Sophie, you read me?"

"Loud and clear Gavin."

"Anything yet on the computers."

"No, but it's only 7 o'clock. Wait a minute. I see two cats at the base of tunnel one."

"Sophie, we hear you. Tell us exactly what you see." Joe said.

"Oh my gosh, get back up here, quick, they are heading your way. Jack, Joe Run. They are running up the tunnel."

"O-k Jack you ready? There are two of them and two of us. We need to kill them and head on out of here and get the rest."

"I'm ready Joe. Let's go get them."

All hell broke loose. Sophie was screaming in their ears to retreat. Jack and Joe pulled out their guns and ran forward a little ways.

"What are you two doing, I said they were coming up the tunnel. You have to get out, now!"

"We here you Soph. But we are here to kill them,

not run from them. Listen; just tell me when they are about 200 yards away. With the curves in the tunnel I don't want to run into them."

"Be careful." Sophie sounded like she was going to cry. It was too much.

The guys slowly walked down the tunnel. Their backs were against the wall. Now they were just waiting.

"O-k, here they come, oh god be careful." Sophie screamed.

Sophie watched on the computer screen. There was a curve in the tunnel and that is where the guys disappeared around the corner. All she could see was dust, and lots of it.

Jack and Joe fired their guns as the cats came around the corner. They hit their mark, two down. They were young, not as big as the others they had encountered. As they headed down the tunnel they had to drag the cats down and out with them.

"You guys o-k?" Gavin asked.

"Yea! Just trying to drag these cats out of the tunnel. We found the smell. A dead possum was in the tunnel. I guess we should have blocked both ends of the tunnel."

"Way to go Joe, We are almost out of tunnel two. Sophie you see anything on our end?" Billy asked.

"You guys are clear in two and three." Sophie radioed back.

Sophie sat back in her chair and took a deep breath. She closed her eyes for a moment and prayed. When she opened her eyes she about jumped out of her skin. Gavin was standing right behind her in the office.

"Where the hell did you come from?" Sophie

shouted at him. Her gun was drawn. "I could have shot you."

"What in your sleep. I came in the kitchen entrance with my remote. You didn't see me on the monitor?"

"I just closed my eyes for a minute." Sophie said.

"Sophie, listen, that one minute could have been a life. You have to keep sharp. I don't want Joe to loose another friend, or his own life."

"What do you mean, who did Joe loose? He would have told us, were his friends." Sophie had tears in her eyes. It was a close call with those cats down there, and she was a nervous wreck. Sophie put the gun away in her holster and sat back down.

"I don't know Sophie; it's really something you should talk to Joe about."

"Gavin, please tell me. What happened?" Sophie begged.

"Sophie, I don't know."

"Please..." Sophie took Gavins hand.

"Alright, but I didn't tell you." Gavin took a deep breath and started. "About six months ago Joe was dating this girl named Andrea. At the time we hadn't figured out all the specifics about these cats and the full moon twist. They had gone into town for dinner. They decided to come back here after dinner and watch a movie. As soon as they got out of the car, a cat jumped them. Joe fought it off the best he could. He didn't have a gun or knife with him. The cat finally ran off. Joe got up and Andrea was laying there in a pool of blood, she was barely breathing. Joe called an ambulance, but as you can imagine it took some time to come up from town. By the time they got up here Andrea had died."

"Oh my...this is terrible. I wonder why he didn't tell us."

"I think it just hurts to bad, he really liked her. I think he was going to propose."

"Oh Gavin, that is so sad. No wonder he wants those cats killed. He does have score to settle."

"Ever since I met Joe all he talks about is you and Jack. I really think he wanted a relationship like yours to complete him."

"You know Gavin, Joe is our best friend, we would do anything for him. I wish we had known, we would have made the trip up here sooner."

"I think he didn't want to burden you. He wanted to get through it, all himself. But now we are all in this together."

"I guess we are." Sophie sighed.

"Look we had better watch these screens." Gavin said.

Gavin and Sophie sat in silence for a while, watching the computer screens. There wasn't much going on, there was no signs of cats.

"Where are they, I don't see the guys or the cats." Sophie said.

"Let's get on the radio's, that's what they are here for.

"Oh yea, I guess my mind is elsewhere." Sophie picked up her radio. "Hey Jack, are you there?"

"Hey babe, we are about at the end of the tunnel."

"All clear, I don't see anything out there yet."

"O-k, we are going to head up towards the compound, if we don't see anything we will be up in the trees. If we do, you will know."

"Billy and Josh, where are yall?" Sophie spoke into the radio.

"Were coming out of tunnel two, heading your way" Josh answered.

"Be careful out there." Sophie said.

Billy and Josh walked towards the compound, Josh climbed up one of the deer stands and played lookout for Billy. Billy walked a few hundred feet and climbed another stand.

Billy got on the radio, "Gage, where are you?"

"Leaving the tunnel now. I am heading back towards the compound."

Joe beeped in, "Be careful, remember those cats are fast, I can't say it enough."

"Yea, I know."

"O-k, I have Joe and Jack on camera, they just left tunnel one." Sophie said.

"Hey, we hear some movement in the woods where the den is." Joe said "We are heading towards the tree line. We may need back up."

"Sophie, this is Gage, Am I clear to move?"

"All clear, where are you going?"

"I'm back up. Keep me posted if you see anything."

"You got it."

Gavin grabbed the radio, "Hey buddy, don't be a hero. If you need help let everyone know and Billy and Josh will back you up."

"Don't worry about that, I've seen these things more than once. I am not going to be their dinner."

Sophie and Gavin continued to watch the computer monitor. As it got darker out the pictures turned a bright green. The night vision cameras were working fine. Sophie clicked on the screen where Joe and

Jack were. The picture became larger. Sophie started to panic again.

She grabbed the radio off the desk, “Jack and Joe, the cats are moving in on your rear, I thought you were supposed to be behind them.”

“It’s o-k, we can hear them, were hidden in the brush. Here they come.”

Sophie watched the screen. There were four cats creeping around. They started towards the compound. One of the cats stopped and lifted his head up into the air. He caught a scent. About the same time Joe saw his head pop up, he fired. Down went the cat. Now the other cats stopped. There was loud screaming off in the woods. The cats went running, they were heading towards the house. Joe and Jack were right behind them now. Gage was behind a tree a few hundred yards up the hill. Jack started shooting. Down went another cat. Joe fired next, he missed, fired again and another one went down. That was three, the forth was running right towards the area where Gage was hiding.

Gage practically whispered in the radio, “You guys listen up, the cat is heading my way, Slow up, I have him.”

“Copy that, there are more heading that way. After we hear the shot, beep me and let me know it’s cool to resume up the hill.”

Shots rang out, Gage hit his mark, beeped the others and he headed up the hill.

Billy and Josh had there own battle going on. A few of the cats were getting close to the compound. Shots rang out from the deer stands, some cats went down, and some kept running.

In the office Sophie and Gavin were watching what they could see. Cats were everywhere now. Some had gotten past the mote and were climbing up to the windows. The stairs were hidden under the house, so all the cats could do is jump up to the window shutters and hold on.

"Sophie I'm going to get rid of some of these cats, watch the screens, and let me know where they are and where they are going."

"O-k, I got it, be careful."

Gavin checked the monitor one last time and saw they were at the front windows; he grabbed his gun and ran to the livingroom. Sticking the gun out of one of the peep holes he started firing.

Sophie screamed from the office. "You got one, keep firing."

Gavin kept firing, moving the gun barrel to the left and then to the right.

"Gavin, go to the side window. There are two over there."

Gavin ran over to the side window and fired away. Down went another one. It was time to reload. He could hear the slamming of the bodies on the shutters.

"Sophie get in here, I need back up. They are at all the windows."

"I'm on my way." Picking up the radio Sophie beeped in to the guys out in the woods. "It looks like we are in trouble here guys, we need help. The cats are at all the windows. I am headed out of the office to help Gavin. There must be 30 or 40 trying to get in."

"We're on our way baby, start shooting, we will keep low, let's go everyone. Billy and Josh, your closer what do you see?" yelled Jack.

"Where heading down from the stands now. It's like a mass exodus from the woods to the compound."

"Jack, hurry! I hear banging in the cellar; they are trying to get through the door down there."

Gage radioed in, "I'm on my way; I will circle around to the trap door and try to get in there. I will kill off anything I can and come in from the cellar."

Billy and Josh had climbed down from the tree stand, and started firing on the cats that were coming up on them. They noticed the traps were knocked over; the formaldehyde was in the air from the broken jars, there was no way of telling if the cats drank the antifreeze that was in the bowls. Some of the cats didn't seem to notice they were standing there, they just headed towards the compound, they were on a mission. Joe and Jack were heading up the hill, killing anything that moved. The screaming was deafening.

Back at the house, the gunfire never stopped. Sophie and Gavin were firing out the peep holes of the shutters.

Gage made it to the back of the house. Crawling on the ground, and firing at the cats was a challenge. He got the job done, made it to the door and engaged the remote. The lock popped open and he entered the cellar. As he went in he closed the door behind him and locked it.

The banging and scratching was loud. It sounded like there was more than one cat inside the cellar. Gage kept his back against the wall. He was following the cellar around to where the door was. The cat or cats were in the tunnel trying to get into the cellar. As Gage came around the corner there were splinters of wood everywhere. The cats had almost made it through the opening. Crouching down with his back against the wall Gage cocked his gun. The first cat came through an opening in the door; it went right towards the stairs. It didn't even see Gage, just passed right by him. The first shot rang out. The first cat went down. The second cat was a little more cautious. He spotted Gage by the wall, and started towards him in a flash. All Gage could hear was a high pitched screaming, he didn't know if it was the cat or himself. He fired his gun and down went the second cat. That was all the cats that had come up the tunnel and into the cellar.

Gage stood up and brushed off his pants. He took a deep breath.

"Hey are you guy's o-k up there?" he radioed in.

Gavin was busy firing at the cats, Sophie picked up her radio, "There are a lot of cats out there, and we need help. I haven't been able to watch the computers, is everything o-k Jack?"

"Were heading towards the compound now. There doesn't seem to be many left." Jack said.

"Sophie," Joe cut in, "Go back to the monitors, Gage will go in the house and help Gavin. I need to know if any more of the cats are coming out of the woods."

"You got it." Sophie ran to the office. All the computers were up and running. She checked each monitor. "Joe, the tunnels are clear as far as I can see. Nothing else is coming out of the woods. I just see a few cats around the compound."

"O-k, thanks, we will get them on the way up. By the way Sophie, Great job, it looks like a war went on up here."

Jack and Joe continued to fire on the cats. There were only two or three left, and they were easy targets. The cats didn't pay attention to who was behind them; they were focused on the house and trying to get in. Shots rang out and down they went.

"Jack, Joe, you got them, looks like all is clear for now."

"Great, I'm bushed, were coming up to the house." Jack said.

As the guys walked up to the house the radio clicked again. "You're not going to believe this, Guess who is here?" Sophie sounded excited.

"You have got to be kidding me, the counties finest, right?"

"You've got it, flashing lights, two cars and four men; they are heading up the hill with guns drawn. I guess someone reported the gun fire."

"Sophie, bring up the shutters for now, we will probably have to bring the good officers in the house." Joe said.

"Good officers my a..."

"Sophie, be nice, at least they finally got here and will be able to see the carnage."

Sophie, Gage and Gavin came out of the house and stool on the porch. It was 9pm and it was getting very cold outside. Billy and Josh were walking over to the house as well as Joe and Jack. The men looked like they had been in a battle. They were dirty, and their clothes and hair was ruffled. But no one was hurt.

There were thirty-five to forty cats lying dead all over the property. The spikes in the mote had captured four.

The four officers walked up the hill towards the compound.

"Looks like we missed all the excitement Joe." Officer James said.

"Yea, if you guys were here about an hour ago you could have helped out, but I guess you were busy. So what brings you up here now?" Joe asked.

"We had some calls about a lot of gunfire, just a few concerned citizens."

"Where is Callahan?"

"He had some other things to take care of tonight. You guys have permits for those guns?" James took out a pad and pen.

"I got permits, I also took care of a bad problem, doesn't this even phase you a bit. Look what has been tormenting me and the people of this mountain. It's not over; they will be back out tomorrow night."

"What do you mean? Looks like you got about 40 of these things."

"They breed; they are hidden in the woods. They need to be hunted down and killed. As I told your department they come out on the full and new moon, and they grow. They are small and cute any other time. Then they grow as large as these cats and they hunt and for some reason they want in MY house. Do you now understand my problem?" Joe was shouting now. The officer backed up a little bit.

"Calm down Joe." Officer lackey stepped up. "What else have you got?"

Joes face turned bright red, his temper was flaring and he was about to let loose. Gage stepped up to the officer.

"So we guess you need more than dead hybrid cats for proof, we got your proof. Come in the house."

Sophie pressed the switch for the stairs and they came down and locked into place. Everyone went into the house.

"I'm going to make some hot coffee, I sure everyone needs it." Sophie left the room and headed towards the kitchen.

"Let's go into the office, that is where command central is set up." Gage led the way into the office.

Officer James and Lackey followed Gage. Billy, Joe, Josh and Jack followed them in. The other officers stood at the front door. Looking out, they could see all the dead cats. They just looked at each other.

Joe started again, "Look guys, we have done everything humanly possible to get rid of these things. You want proof, here it is. We have video feed, we have one of Sloan's journals, we even have body parts in jars. We just found them; they were hidden behind a fake wall in the cellar."

"What do you mean Sloans Journal?" James asked.

"We found it inside a pile of material in one of the closets in the lab."

"You have a lab?" Lackey asked.

"No, I don't have a lab, Sloan had a lab. Look if you guys can't help me I am calling the media. I have spent thousands of dollars to try and get rid of this problem. Every month they come back in numbers. They want something here. I don't know what, but I have been through this house with a fine tooth comb."

"Whoa there Joe, we don't want the media involved in this, it would just scare the town's people and cause real problems."

Joe got up in the officers face. Gage stood up and walked towards them. The officer backed up a bit and placed his hand on his gun holster.

"I don't care. You get it, I want help now!" Joe said.

Gage put his hand on Joe's shoulder. "Come on Joe, let's show them the cellar."

As they walked out of the office Billy walked over to the other two officers. "The night is still young, if you see any of these cats, shoot to kill, or they may kill you. They are fast." He flipped the switch to the stairs and they disappeared up and into the bottom of the house.

Billy walked into the kitchen and sat down.

"You want a cup of coffee Billy?" Sophie asked.

"Sure, it looks like we are going to be up all night anyway. You did a great job tonight Sophie. I glad we have you on our side. I am wondering about those officers."

"What do you mean?"

"I think they want to hide all this for another reason, I just can't figure out what."

"They may just want to keep peace in the town. People would get scarred and leave, it would become a ghost town if that happened."

"I think that is a little far fetched. If they would just come out here and help us, we could get rid of them all. We got a lot tonight, no telling how many are going to come out tomorrow night."

Jack and Gavin came into the kitchen for coffee. Josh stayed in the office watching the computer monitors.

Sophie poured coffee for everyone and then left the room to bring a cup to Josh. She set it down on the desk and turned to leave.

"Wait Sophie, Thanks for the coffee. Come here a

minute. What do you see right here?" Josh was pointing to the monitor.

"With the flashing lights of the patrol cars I can't tell. What do you see?"

"Look right here," Josh pointed to the opening on tunnel one.

"Oh crap, it looks like we have more visitors. There's maybe about three or four of them. You had better radio Joe and Gage. I will go and get the guys." Sophie ran frome the room.

Josh picked up his radio and called the guys in the cellar." Get ready guys, we have three to four cats heading your way. Watch out for tunnel one. We are sending down reinforcement now."

"You have got to be kidding. Shit." Joe informed the officer and Gage what was going on.

The cellar door opened, the other two officers and Gavin went running down the stairs. Gage and Joe were shouting instructions.

"Lackey, you and Gage go to either side of the tunnel. Gavin, use the stairs for cover. James, stand on the stairs with your men. Remember these things are fast. One blink of the eye and they are on top of you. Shoot to kill!"

Joe's radio beeped. "There heading your way, I see three. Jack is upstairs watching out the windows." Sophie said.

"Thanks Sophie, We got it from here, just watch the house."

The cats creeped down the tunnel, they were slowing down. Joe and the others didn't know it but the cats had drank the antifreeze, they were dying inside.

"Joe they are almost there. It's really strange, they are slow." Sophie reported.

"What do you mean, slow?" Joe asked.

"Just what I said, they are coming around the corner now. Get ready, NOW!" Sophie screamed.

The cats creeped slowly around the corner. The moaning constant and slow. The first cat made it around the corner. Office Lackey fired on the animal. Down it went.

"Hold your fire." Joe screamed. "Somethings not right."

"Look at that thing." Lackey cried. "What do you mean, hold your fire?"

"These cats are very fast. This one that just came around the corner was slow, which means they got into the antifreeze." Joe beeped Sophie on the radio. "Where are the others? Only one cat came through the tunnel into the cellar."

"Joe, I don't see them, they must be in the turn. They haven't come out yet?"

"I'll get back with you." Joe turned to Gage and Gavin. "Come on, we have to see where they are."

The three of them went into the tunnel. The officers followed at a good distance behind. The all walked slowly waiting for something to jump out at them. Nothing happened. Then there was a most terrible noise. It was a scream and a moan all in one.

"Look, there they are, and they look like they are dead or dying. It must have been the antifreeze." Joe said.

Officer James spoke up, "What do you keep talking about, what's with the antifreeze?"

"Antifreeze is lethal, animals are attracted to it,

they drink it and then they die. We set traps outside, and it looks like it worked, for now anyway. We still have to get through tomorrow night." Joe explained.

"I thought you said they only came out once a month?" Lackey asked.

"They do, but for two nights, the full moon and the new moon. Tomorrow night will be worse because there is no natural light. It will be pitch black out there." Joe looked at the officers. "Can we count on your help? We are going to need all the help we can get."

Officer James looked at Lackey, "I'm in, I'm sure if we report what we've seen tonight, Callahan will send out all the officers he can."

Joe nodded, "Thanks, we are starting early in the morning."

"Yea, we have to get rid of the bodies and reset the traps. I hope ya'll can bring shovels and be here early in the morning." Gage said.

"Hey James, Can we get a garbage truck here first thing in the morning? If we can we won't have to dig holes and bury them, it will take a lot less time. Then we can concentrate on setting more traps and reloading." Gage looked exhausted.

Joe beeped Jack, "Hey buddy, you see anything else out there?"

"No, we haven't seen anything else since the cats in the tunnel, I think we are done for tonight."

"Well, I don't trust them, so keep up the security measures. Disengage the stairs and we will be right up."

Everyone went up the stairs and into the kitchen. Sophie had made fresh coffee and grilled cheese sandwiches. Joe grabbed a cup off the counter and poured himself a cup. The others followed. As they ate and drank their coffee, they talked about what needed to be done tomorrow. Officer James was on the phone talking to Callahan and the other officers were taking notes.

Joe stood up and started pacing around the kitchen. He topped off his coffee, and then sat back down.

Gavin spoke up first, "Joe tonight went pretty well, huh?"

"Yea, we got a lot of them, I just wonder what is going to happen tomorrow night."

"Me too." Billy said. "So what is the plan for tomorrow?"

"The same as today. We have to reinforce the door in the cellar again. That cat tore it up pretty good." Joe said.

"I guess we have to set up the bowls of formaldehyde in the traps and check the deer stands." Billy stood up and stretched.

"I think I am going to hit the sack, it's been a long day." Sophie stood up and Jack followed her towards the stairs.

"Night you guys, see ya in the AM." Jack called out.

The rest of the guys stayed in the living room for a little while and talked. After a while the conservation came to a lull. One by one they stretched out on the couch or in a sleeping bag on the floor and went to sleep. Joe got up and went to his room and crashed in the bed.

34

The moon was full. The humans were asleep. The cats were not. They were roaming in the night, migrating to the compound and studying their dead. All was quiet. The smell of blood and chemicals was everywhere. The outside of the compound was in shambles.

As if in a trance, the cats started moving towards the house. They formed a line in front of the house, facing the house, and then they sat down and stared forward. Not a movement from any of them.

After an hour of sitting, and staring, in formation they stood up. Like soldiers they marched to the left and then to the right. Abruptly they stopped, all at once there was the call they were known for, the screaming and moaning coming from twenty of the cats at once. Birds woke up from their sleep and scattered in the air. Larger animals jumped up and ran through the woods. Lights in the distance, that couldn't be seen from the compound, came on. Apart from the night the mountain came alive.

35

All the lights in the house came on. The night before, Joe made sure the shutters were down and the stairs were up. The spikes in the mote were still engaged and the mote was full of water. He looked at the clock and it read three am. He jumped out of bed and ran into the livingroom. The guys were already looking out the peep holes. Jack and Sophie were running down the stairs.

"What is going on?" Sophie asked.

"I don't know, this has never happened before." Joe answered.

Billy moved away from the window, "Yea, but we have never killed so many of them in one night. I am going in the office and check out the computer monitors."

Joe got up and followed him, "Good idea. I'm right behind you."

The two of them left the livingroom and went to the office. The computers were left on from the night before. Josh, Gage and Gavin stayed in the livingroom watching out the peep holes. Sophie picked up the blanket on the couch, folded it and laid it across the back of the couch. Sophie was one to keep busy. The guys were watching the cats and the cats were watching the house.

Jack was the only one still sleeping. Sophie told people he could sleep through a tornado. Sophie walked upstairs to check on him.

Back in the office Joe and Billy were watching the cats.

"Why are they just sitting there?" Billy asked Joe.

"I don't know, but, I think now would be a good time to line up at the peep holes and shoot as many of them as we can."

"Good idea, let's tell the others."

They left the office and went into the livingroom.

"Pull out your guns guys; we are going to get in some target practice." Joe said.

There was a smile on everyones face. Everyone pulled out their guns and went to the windows. Guns were set up and the firing began. When the first shot rang out the cats scattered. They kept shooting. It was only two minutes later and the ones they shot were dead; the others ran off into the woods.

"That was so strange. Why would they line up like that?" Gavin asked.

"Who knows, is there anything normal about these creatures?" Gage answered.

Sophie and Jack came down the stairs. In the livingroom everyone was sitting down and trying to come up with an explanation of what was going on.

"I'm going back to bed; I have got to be fresh for tomorrow." Joe got up and left the room.

Sophie and Jack talked with the guys for a few minutes and went back to bed.

"I think someone should watch the monitors the rest of the night." Billy suggested.

"We really need our rest for tomorrow." Josh said.

Gage stood up, "I think we should take shifts, I'll take the first shift. You guys go and get some rest. If these things start to come back, I want to be ready."

The guys went and layed down. Gage went to the office and sat in front of the monitors. At five Gage started to dose off. He got up and let Gavin know he was going to sleep for a couple of hours, and not to worry about his shift, Nothing was going on outside. Gage layed down and went to sleep.

36

At 8am Joe got up and took his shower. He got dressed and went into the kitchen. Sophie was already up and making coffee. The others were getting up, taking showers and getting dressed. Joe poured himself a cup of coffee and sat down at the table.

"Your up and busy." Joe said.

"I was up a lot earlier, I just layed in bed for about an hour, I couldn't sleep."

"I know the feeling, that was so weird this morning. I have never seen the cats act that way." Joe got up and started pulling out the cereal boxes and bowls out of the cabinet.

"Joe, I can make breakfast for everyone if you want."

"Cereal is fine." Joe pulled the milk out of the refrigerator. "We need to get ready for our day; I have a feeling its going to be a long one."

Joe's cell phone started ringing, "Hello, yea, we are o-k in here. I will open the shutters, stay right there."

Joe went over to the bank of switches on the wall, and flipped the switches to let the stairs down and the shutters up. He went in the livingroom to the front door. Officers Lackey and James were standing on the front stoop. Joe opened the door and let them in.

Gage, Gavin, Billy and Josh were finishing getting ready and went to the kitchen to eat and get coffee. Jack came down the stairs and joined them.

Officer Lackey spoke first, "Joe, the neighbors were calling the station last night, we must have had ten calls about screaming and gun fire. What the hell was going on?"

"It was the strangest thing, about three am the cats lined up in front of the house; they just sat there and screamed. We all jumped up and saw them, so we started firing on them. We have to get rid of them."

"Well, we are here to help. The garbage truck is down at the end of the hill. That is about all Callahan can offer right now."

"Did you tell him about last night? Did you make it clear to him what a problem this was?" Joe was a little frustrated.

"Yea, but we are short handed down in town. Me and James were supposed to be off today, we volunteered to help out. This is just too crazy to miss, plus we get to shoot something. There's not much action in this little town." Lackey said.

Joe just laughed, "I guess your right. Well I guess I will take all the help we can get."

Joe went to the kitchen where the others were finishing up. They were talking about the events of last night. Sophie was loading the dishes in the dishwasher.

"Well guys," Joe said. "Are we ready for today?"

Gavin stood up, "Ready as ever, I'm just glad after tonight it will be over for a month."

"Me too," Gage said, "Maybe I will get some sleep

and be able to enjoy my retirement."

Billy laughed, "You poor guy, must be nice to retire at thirty."

"It is, you should try it." Gage looked over to Joe, "So I guess we should start cleaning up the compound while we have the trash truck here."

"Yea, but some one needs to stay here and watch the monitors."

"I will stay; I can't deal with death and the smell." Sophie volunteered.

Jack spoke up, "Oh, so now you don't want to be Ms. Rambo, that's convenient."

"Great idea Sophie, you keep an eye on the compound, and the woods surrounding it. We will have our radios and guns. At the first sign of anything, just let us know.

Sophie finished cleaning up the kitchen and went into the office. She sat down in front of the computers and played with the zoom feature.

They guys were suiting up to go out and dispose of the bodies. They checked their guns and ammo, and put fresh batteries in the radios.

Jack went into the office to say goodbye to Sophie.

"Hey babe, where is your gun and ammo?"

"Oh, let me run up and get it."

Sophie left the office and ran up the stairs to get her gun. Jack watched the monitors till she returned a few minutes later.

"O-k I am ready. You be careful out there. I love you."

"Love you too. Let us know if you see anything, and we will be back in a couple of hours."

Jack left the office and joined the others. Joe was handing out Heavy gloves, he handed Jack a pair.

"Alright guys," Joe said, "this is not going to be fun. These cats are big, and they stink. There are a couple of wheel barrows around the back of the house, we will get those and we can put some in the back of the tractor. The rest we will have to drag."

Billy cut in, "Joe, do you have any Vicks vapor rub?"

"Yea, what for?" Joe asked.

"If you put it under your noses, you won't be able to smell the cats much. It's a little trick I learned from my wife, she used to work at the animal clinic in town." Billy said.

Joe went into his bathroom and got the Vicks. When he came out he passed it around and everyone put some under their noses.

"Well, let's get started." Joe said.

Everyone went out the door and down the stairs. There were dead cats everywhere. The smell of death, and rotting flesh was in the air. Blood was all over the place, on the trees and on the ground. The guys went around to get the wheel barrows and the tractor. As they started towards the front of the house, they loaded the bodies up one by one. The hardest part was pushing them down the hill to the garbage truck.

The truck driver sat in the truck; he didn't want anything to do with what was happening. He layed is seat back and closed his eyes.

"Man, this is hard work." Jack complained.

"Yea, I know, unfortunately I haven't grated out a driveway yet. That's next on the list." Joe said. "By the way, Jack, Thank you for helping out. There's nothing like having your friends around to help you out of a hard situation."

It took two hours to remove the thirty five dead animals from the compound. Before the truck left, Joe gave the driver a hundred dollar bill. The guy looked sick but happy to get some extra cash. As the garbage truck left the mountain, there was a loud scream coming from the woods. The guys stopped and looked around and then at each other.

"Let's get back to the house." Josh said. He started back up the hill.

The officers followed everyone back up the house. Even though it was day light, everyone was cautious about their surroundings. The cats were out there. Joe and his friends knew it.

Jacks radio beeped. "Jack, I see you guys are heading back, how did it go?'

"It sucked. Those suckers were heavy. I'll see you in ten minutes."

"See ya then." Sophie said.

After everyone got back to the house, they cleaned up a bit then met in the office. Jack watched the computers while Sophie went and got some coffee.

37

"So what's the plan for the rest of the day?" Josh asked.

Joe stood up and paced the office floor. "Well, we have to fix the door in the cellar, replace the ammo in the deer stands and set the antifreeze bowls out again. That's about it."

"You guys want to split up?" Gage asked.

Sophie came back into the room and sat down, "I tell you what, you guys do that and watch the monitor and I will go and make a real good meal for later on. I am tired of soup and sandwiches."

"O-k, Jack you stay in this time and keep look out. Gage and Gavin, take Lackey with you and stock the stands, and set out the antifreeze while you are out there, then you can come back and help us in the cellar. James you can come with me, Billy and Josh down to the cellar."

"Uh, Joe, I think you may want to take a look at this." Jack said.

On the monitor there were six cats entering the cellar. They were just walking up the tunnel like they had all day. Joe, Jack and the others just watched them. The looked over to the other screens and there were no cats anywhere else, just these six walking slowly up the tunnel.

"Come on; let's get them before they reach the cellar." Joe said. He got up and headed towards the kitchen.

Officer James, Billy and Josh followed Joe into the kitchen and down the stairs. As soon as the cellar door was shut, Sophie locked it.

They were a few steps down the stairs when they saw it. There were at least twelve cats at the bottom of the stairs, they were lying down, with there heads up just watching the humans descend the stairwell. The guys turned and ran up the stairs. Joe was screaming for Sophie to open the door. One of the cats jumped up and headed up the stairs after them.

Sophie opened the door and the four of them practically tumbled in the kitchen door screaming to shut the door. As the door slammed the cat hit it with full force. Then came the screaming again. From the cellar the sound vibrated off the walls, the whole house shook.

"Crap that was close. Sophie, how did those cats get in the cellar with out you seeing them?" Joe asked.

"I don't know, I watched the monitors the whole time. I didn't see anything." Sophie said.

Jack came running into the kitchen, "What happened, those cats are still in the tunnel. They are getting closer."

Joe, Billy and Josh just looked at Jack and then at each other.

"Jack, you didn't see any of the cats already in the cellar? You didn't just see what happened?" Joe screamed, "What are you trying to do kill us?"

"What are you talking about?" Jack asked.

About that time Josh and Billy went running into

the office. On the monitors they watched the six cats coming up the tunnel. At the end of the tunnel there were six more walking into the tunnel. When they looked at the screen where the inside of the cellar was, it showed an empty cellar.

Josh sat down and started banging on the keys. The bank of computers was frozen. The picture on the screen was from earlier in the day. Everyone was gathered around Josh, just watching. After about ten minutes of hitting the keys and doing some reprograming a new screen popped up. It was a frightening sight. There were twenty cats in the cellar. All of them were lying down, facing the stairs.

"What the hell!" Gage gasped.

"Josh, what happened to the computer?" Joe asked.

"I wish I knew, it looks like it just froze up. It's fixed now." Gage looked at the guys. "Anyone have a plan? Looks like we have more visitors coming up the pike."

"Crap, this is not right; they don't come out during the day, how come now?" Joe asked sounding very fustrated.

There was a beep, Joe and Josh looked over towards Officer James. He was on his radio. "Sheriff, we really need back up here at the compound. There are about twenty to thirty cats in the cellar of Joe's place."

On the other end they heard, "What, I thought you guys had this under control?" The sheriff sounded irritated.

"We did, until now. If you don't send up some help, the media will be notified, shiriff, you gotta send some help. If the Media gets involved people are going to get hurt. Send help now!" James said.

"Now son, are you giving me orders?" The shiriff said.

"Yes sir! I'm with them. These things are mean. Get the ranger to call Joe on his cell, get animal control to call me on mine. This is out of hand."

"Your out of line son, I make these decisions, not you!" The shiriff yelled into the radio.

Officer James looked over to Joe. "I guess we have to do what we have to do."

"Gage, call the forest ranger. Gavin, make the call to the media. I will call Animal control." Joe said.

Officer Lackey put his police radio down and dialed a number on his private cell phone. When the F.B.I. picked up, he informed them of the problem and what his superior officer had to say about it.

Billy and Josh watched the monitors while the calls were being made. The cats kept entering the tunnel on one end and coming into the cellar on the other end.

"Gage got off the phone with forest ranger. "He is teaming up with animal control, there going to try to go around the cats and get to the compound from the top of the hill."

"The media is on the way, I told them what they needed to know to be safe." Gavin said.

"O-k here is the plan" Lackey said, "The beaureu is contacting the ranger. They are basically taking over. Sorry Joe, we have to sit tight." Lackey said.

"To hell with that, those things are in my house. Can't we throw down tear gas or something, when they leave the tunnell we can be waiting for them?" Joe said.

"Sounds like a good plan to me," Gage said, "I am ready to blow them up."

Lackey spoke up, "There are not enough of us. We need people at all three tunnels. They will scatter if we do that."

"Your right. We need to wait on back up. James, you look a little worried, I hope you didn't just get yourself fired." Joe said

"Whatever, I hope Callahan gets himself fired. He sits on his fat ass and does nothing but order us around. I think he is worried about the re-election."

"Yea, that is coming up." Josh said.

An hour later, there where helecoptors in the air and there were people knocking on the door. The cellar filled up with the creatures, they were lying on the ground, watching the door.

Sophie opened the front door. Several members of Park services and the F.B.I. were standing at the door. She let them in the house. The helecoptors were in the air.

Josh was at the computer monitors, a media van pulled up in the parking area. No one got out because there were a couple of the large cats standing outside the tunnel. It looked like they were standing guard.

Animal control showed up thirty minutes later.

Everyone gathered in the living room. One of the F.B.I. agents stood up and walked to the center of the room. He cleared his throat and everyone got quiet.

"My name is Agent Ledbetter. I am with the Federal Beareau of Investigations. Your friend Gage happens to be a friend of mine from way back. We are here to help with this problem. I have seen the tapes of the cats. I have been watching the monitors with Josh and Billy. These things look mean and we need to distroy them. Let's get started. We are going to break up in to groups. Gage will take one group down the hill to that tunnel. Gavin will take a group up the hill, he knows the area. Joe will take the third group out towards the east tunnel. We need people up in the deer stands. Sophie and Jack are keeping tabs on the monitors. Josh, you and Billy and the officers will stay here.

Mr. Martin from park services is going to let off tear gas into the cellar. We hope that will disperse the cats, we want them to leave the cellar and the tunnels, when they come out, the teams will fire on them."

Joe looked over to Officer Lackey and winked; the officer smiled and rolled his eyes.

Ledbetter looked around, "Are there any questions?"

Gage spoke up, "We have our radios, and I think it would be a good idea to sinc up before we go out."

"Good idea." Joe said.

"What channel are you guys on?" Ledbetter asked.

"Were on channel twenty seven, and just in case we need to change over, our back up is thirty two." Gage said.

"Great, let's go play boys!"

Everyone got up and met up in their teams, Gage and his guys were the first to leave. Gavin and Joe's team left next. Jack and Sophie went into the office and sat down. They were instructed to watch the teams and when everyone was in position, to let the ranger know. He would then set off the tear gas. Sophie would tell each team that the cats were on their way down the tunnel.

Josh, Billy and the Officers hung out by the windows, watching and waiting.

In the office Sophie and Jack watched all the men going their separate ways. They had to reach the end of each tunnel and position themselves in a good spot to get a good shot at the cats. After twenty five minutes Joe and his team were in position. Five minutes after that Gavins team showed up near tunnel two. It took Gage and his team another five minutes. Everyone was in place.

Sophie yelled to Mr Martin, "Everyone is in place." Then she let the teams know he was about to drop the gas. "Hey guys, Martin is going to drop the tear gas in two minutes."

The guys checked in, everyone was ready. Ledbetter went to the cellar door with Martin. Lackey and James were right behind them. They needed to be ready just in case one or more of the cats were on the steps. With guns drawn Martin opened the door just enough to drop the tear gas. Martin dropped the gas and slammed the door and locked it.

The cats started screaming. The sound shook the house. Everyone covered their ears. Jack and Sophie watched as the cats scattered to the tunnels. They were bumping into each other, the tear gas blurrerd their vision, and burned their noses.

"O-k guys here they come, and watch out, they're in a lot of pain." Sophie watched, within minutes, the cats were piling out of the tunnels. As soon as they hit the ground the men were firing at them. One by one they went down.

Joe and his team killed ten of the cats; they were piled up outside the tunnel like trash. When the cats quit coming out of the tunnel the team went in. They were taking no prisioners; they all had to be put to death. The closer they got to the cellar the stonger the gas smell was. They couldn't go in all the way.

Gavin's group got fifteen coming out of two. After waiting to see if any more were coming out they too went in as far as they cold go, they found no more cats.

Gage and his guys were waited a little longer than the rest of the men. Tunnel one was the main tunnel, the first tunnel to have the cats venture up it. After waiting a good amount of time, up the tunnel they went. There were no more cats coming down. They went back out of the tunnel.

Joe's radio beeped, and well as Gavin's and Gages. "Hey, Ledbetters men are going down into the cellar, they have masks on. Stay at the end of your tunnels. They are going to make the trip down the tunnel to see if there are any cats hiding and flush them out."

"You got it." Joe radioed back.

Ledbetter had three men going down each tunnel. Because of the masks and the remnents of the tear gas it was hard to see. They didn't know what to expect so they took it slow.

The guys were waiting when the men came out the end of the tunnels. No other cats came out before them.

Sophie radioed to them, "Everyone alright?"

"We are, just tired, what's happening up at the house?" Joe asked.

"No cats came out up here at the compound, and we don't see any on the monitors. All is clear for now. Stay alert on you way back up here." Jack said.

"Alright we are on our way back."

The rest of the men checked in and were on their way back to the compound. Some of the media stayed at the end of the tunnels taking pictures and film of the dead cats. Camera crews and news men and women treaked up the hill after the men, they were asking questions. Gage and Gavin informed the media all questions would be answered when they got back to the compound. Joe on the other hand, did answer some of the questions. He was tired of being put off by the county shiriffs office and wanted the world to know about it.

Back at the compound, Jack stayed in the office while Sophie went into the kitchen and made coffee. After she got that started she cut up some cheese and made a tray of cheese and crackers. If everyone was as hungry as she was this would help. Sophie grabbed the chips and salsa off the counter and set up the table in the dining room with munchies for everyone.

The men started coming in from their trek in the woods. They looked tired and thirsty. The officers that had stayed at the house served the men coffee and sodas. Joe and his friends went into the office and shut the door.

"Well, that was successful." Josh said.

"It's about time we got some help. I am wondering how many more there are out there." Joe sat down in the chair in front of the computer screens. He tapped the mouse, thinking. "We need to get ready for tonight. I need some suggestions. We have to get the rest of these things by tonight. Or next month we will have another battle on our hands."

Gage stood up, "I think while it is still light out, we

should get teams out in the woods and scour the areas we know that they hide. Take as many out before dark as we can. We also need to set guards up at the opening of each tunnel so that none of the cats can get back in. I think two men each will do."

"Great thinking Gage, we have enough help now, we can put a couple of guys in each deer stand also." Joe said.

Billy got up and headed for the door, "Well, let's get on the ball, we only have a couple of hours before dark."

Everyone got up except Jack, he was going to stay and monitor the computers with Sophie.

"Jack, I want the thank you again for staying. You have been a great help to me and my friends." Joe walked over and shook Jacks hand.

"No problem Joe, I am just glad no one has gotten hurt. Those cats scare the hell out of me."

Joe left the office and went into the livingroom area where everyone was hanging out. It was a small room that seemed smaller with so many people in it. He walked over to Agent Ledbetter and stood beside him. Sophie brought him coffee and he thanked her.

Joe cleared his throat, "Excuse me, can I have everyones attention?" Everyone got quiet. "First I want to thank you for your help. My friends and I have been battling these things for several months now, I am hopeing after tonight the battle will be over. We still have a little work to do. Tonight is the new moon. If there are still cats out there we need to get them. When the sun goes down they will reach their full potentail, and if you thought they were mean today, you really don't want to see them tonight."

Ledbetter spoke up, "What do you mean tonight? I thought we were done here.

"No, but I hope not far from it. Up until yesterday and today, the cats never came out during the day, only at night. And when they came out it was with a vengence. We need to get outside and hunt them down. The ones that are left are probley pissed off. It would be much better if we can see them in the day light and get rid of them. So if you, Agent Ledbetter would organize your men, I will get mine and the officers ready. We need to go out in groups of no less than three. Scour the wooded area just beyound the trees. Shoot to kill men. Sophie and Jack will be on the radios, remember when they speak, everyone can hear what is going on. Be alert, no matter how big or small they are, we have to kill them all."

Joe sent Gage and Gavin to one of the deer stands and Billy and Josh to another. The two officers from county along with two of the rangers went down the hill to the base of tunnel one. Before they left, he showed them on the map where the cats come out at. He then helped the agent get his men out the door. After everyone was doing the job they had been assigned to he sat down with his coffee.

Ledbetter sat across from Joe, "So how long have you been dealing with this?"

"About six months now. I have been trying to get help from county for about four. They didn't believe me, or want to believe me."

"I wonder why?" the agent said.

"Who knows, I am just glad you guys showed up to help. Hopefully we can get all of them by tonight and be done with this."

About the time Joe finished his sentence, there was a knock at the door, he got up and opened the door to no less than ten media cameras and reporters. They were crammed on the porch. Joe turned and looked at the agent; he shook his head and invited them all in the house. Everyone started talking at once, throwing questions out and butting in front of each other.

Joe quieted everyone down. "If everyone will just be quiet I will give a statement, and then if you still have questions, we will answer them."

Joe started at the beginning, and told them the story. Everyone sat quietly, other than Joe's voice, the only noise was the clicking of the cameras.

Outside they kept hearing gunfire. There were more of the cats being hunted down. The reporters inside wished they were outside. They did have teams out there, but they all wanted the good action.

The sun was beginning to set. The reporters went back outside to see if there was anything else they could see. It all got very quiet. Joe walked into the office where Jack and Sophie were watching the screens.

"Call everyone in, it's getting dark and I don't want anyone to get hurt. Besides I am sure everyone needs to re-group on ammo and get something on their stomachs."

"Joe, while I was in the kitchen a while ago I started a big pot of Chili. So when they come in they can eat."

"Thanks Soph, I am starving.

Joe left the office and went to get some dinner. The men started coming back to the house.

The sun was setting fast. Everyone had come back. They were swaping stories about what they killed and how many there were out there. Between everyone, Joe counted another fifteen cats.

'How many more can there be' Joe thought.

38

As the sun was setting behind the mountain, the darkness creeped up in the sky. Some of the men were sitting on the porch, but most were inside finishing up Chili and crackers.

Then there it was, the blood curdling scream. The guys that were outside went into the house and shut the door. Joe came in the livingroom from the office and locked the door. He flipped the switch for the shutters and they came down with a slam. Joe checked the other switches. The motes swords were up, and the water was on. He switched the stairs to come up and go under the porch.

"O-k men, we could only see a couple of the cats on the monitors. Usually there are multiple screams about sundown. So far we have only heard one. Maybe this is a good sign. With the shutters down, the windows can be pulled up. Watch out the peep holes. And fire at will."

Joe went back into the office. Sophie and Jack were searching the screens for more cats.

"Joe we only see the two." Sophie said.

"Well keep watch. It only takes two to make hundreds. As soon as they get close enough to fire on, there dead." Joe left the office.

As he approached the kitchen he heard a sound in the cellar. Something was breaking glass; at least that was what it sounded like. No one had been down there since this afternoon. Sophie nor Jack had said anything about any cats getting into the tunnel. About that time Jack came running out of the office yelling for Joe. At the same time Joe had drawn his gun and opened the cellar door and started down the stairs. Gage got up from his chair and rushed to the door and followed Joe. Jack came around the corner and saw the two going down. He screamed for them to stop.

"Joe, Gage there are two cats down there!" Jack yelled.

About that time he heard screaming, it was the cats. Then Joe and Gage were yelling and firing their guns at the cats. Jack went running down the stairs. Joe was screaming for Jack to go back up the stairs. Jack didn't here him. When Jack came around the corner he saw flashes from the gun fire. Gage shot one of the cats and it went down. Joe fired at the other but missed. As Jack stood there watching, the cat that Joe missed leaped into the air and as it landed on Jack. Joe fired again, but not soon enough. The cat had his claws in Jacks chest. There was screaming coming from the cat and Jack. Another shot rang out and the cat fell dead on top of Jack. Joe and Gage went running to Jack. Sophie rounded the corner and over to Jack, She was now screaming. Running over to him she grabbed the cat's skin and fur and pulled at it. The cat was very heavy. Joe and Gage ran over to help. The claws of the cat were stuck in Jack. As Joe and Gage pulled, Sophie pried the claws from Jack. Blood was pouring; Joe ripped off his shirt and told

Sophie to apply pressure while he radioed for help.

The Agent told Joe he watched the whole thing on the computer and had already called for an ambulance.

Billy and Josh went down and helped Joe put Jack on an old door and carry him up the stairs. Sophie was crying and trying to get Jack to wake up.

While all that was going on, the men in the living room hit their marks outside, they got the two cats that made it to the compound. There were no more cats to be seen.

In the distance there were the sounds of sirens.

39

Sophie and Joe were at Jacks bedside when he woke up from surgery. As his eyes opened Sophie leaned down and kissed him. Her tears were streaming down her face and on to his.

Jack looked past Sophie and pointed to Joe. Sophie rose up and looked where Jack was pointing.

"So Joe, where will our next adventure be?"

Everyone laughed; Joe went over and hugged Jack.

40

Back at the compound the officers, the FBI and the park services helped Billy, Josh, Gavin and Gage clean up. During the night all was quiet in the mountains of Tennessee. All the cats were dead.

Except one.